Michael Green is a Canadian author who is currently not sure how he got into this situation. What situation? Any of them! He is known for his enthusiastic love of collecting rocks and shiny things and has a serious stuffed animal problem. He enjoys staying at home with his cats and has a passion for starting craft projects he is well aware that he will never finish, and he is quite surprised this book was able to get done in the first place.

Thank you very much to all who supported and encouraged me as I was writing this book.

Michael Green

HUMAN ADJACENT

AUSTIN MACAULEY PUBLISHERS
LONDON * CAMBRIDGE * NEW YORK * SHARJAH

Copyright © Michael Green 2025

All rights reserved. No part of this publication may be reproduced, distributed, or transmitted in any form or by any means, including photocopying, recording, or other electronic or mechanical methods, without the prior written permission of the publisher, except in the case of brief quotations embodied in critical reviews and certain other non-commercial uses permitted by copyright law. For permission requests, write to the publisher.

Any person who commits any unauthorized act in relation to this publication may be liable to criminal prosecution and civil claims for damages.

This is a work of fiction. Names, characters, businesses, places, events, locales, and incidents are either the products of the author's imagination or used in a fictitious manner. Any resemblance to actual persons, living or dead, or actual events is purely coincidental.

Ordering Information
Quantity sales: Special discounts are available on quantity purchases by corporations, associations, and others. For details, contact the publisher at the address below.

Publisher's Cataloging-in-Publication data
Green, Michael
Human Adjacent

ISBN 9798889105916 (Paperback)
ISBN 9798889105923 (Hardback)
ISBN 9798889105930 (ePub e-book)

Library of Congress Control Number: 2024916147

www.austinmacauley.com/us

First Published 2025
Austin Macauley Publishers LLC
40 Wall Street, 33rd Floor, Suite 3302
New York, NY 10005
USA

mail-usa@austinmacauley.com
+1 (646) 5125767

Table of Contents

Sewn Tight	9
Angler	22
Light of the Divine	27
An Open Letter	41
Eyes Are Windows	57
Made of Stone	65
Calm Waters	79
Soul	93
Death and Taxes	100

Sewn Tight

Emery slowly poked his head into the workshop, keeping his eyes on his work partner as he tried to creep up behind him. It was hard to do on metal limbs, but Emery had been practicing for years. His thundering footsteps always disturbed the workshop's other occupant, so he learned to be quieter. Kinch's scowl was a sound he was very familiar with, years into their partnership. Unlike Emery, Kinch was relatively soft-spoken and quite irritable at everything around him, most of all Emery. He was used to it by now but was still cautious each time he approached. They existed in a tentative state of agreement, in which one could not work without the other, but Kinch absolutely loathed him.

The workshop was a good mess of clutter. Well, Emery's half was. Tools, spare parts, and half-finished blueprints were crammed into every single space available. The floor-to-ceiling wooden shelves were disorganized, the tool benches weren't labeled, and the drawers hadn't closed in years. Emery was horrible at making sure everything was put into place, but it had gotten to the point where he couldn't find anything if it wasn't exactly where he expected it to be, so the screwdrivers stuck out of a flower vase that had never had any flowers in it, and the spools of wire were in a pile on the floor. Scrap metal was shoved into the wooden cubby holes, relying on Emery's mind alone to keep track of them.

Kinch didn't like it, or perhaps he just didn't like it because it was Emery's space. He wanted to work, to invent as Emery did, but that was not his job. Kinch was a tailor, and he was good at what he did. The things he made were always sturdy, yet fashionable, and Emery was thankful for good work clothes and was always saddened when he got grease and oil on them. Kinch's own workstation was neatly covered in different fabrics, the shelves tidied and kept that way. Emery often thought of making him a proper sewing machine so he didn't have to do everything by hand, but he figured it wouldn't be worth the trouble if Kinch couldn't operate it in the first place.

Emery stood a good few feet behind Kinch's chair, waiting for Kinch to notice him. Kinch was slender, light. The complete opposite of what Emery was. He watched taunt stitches in fabric pull as Kinch moved, the navy blue of the thread standing out against white linens. The colored patterns across the fabric were of a lovely variety of flowers, the names of which Emery did not know but was doubtlessly fascinated by the way the hues blended together—deep reds and light blues and the green stems that tied the whole picture together. Often, he would stare at Kinch's back when his partner was not aware of him, tracing the patterns with his eyes to see where they would go. His curiosity was usually cut off by a stem leading underneath Kinch's bright yellow dress, and he could no longer follow it.

"Take a picture," Kinch scowled, still facing the wall, arms placed on his workbench, leaned forward, propped up on his elbows to keep himself from just falling flat on his face. He was in the same position he had been in last night. Of course he was. "It'll last longer."

"I'm sorry," Emery said, his free hand rubbing at his wrist and trying not to wince at the loud screech of metal on metal. He could feel Kinch's anger spike again. He always felt like he needed to apologize to Kinch. His partner hated unnecessary noise, and that was all Emery seemed to be. "I just wanted to get your opinion on something I'm working on."

"Go away."

"It's very important," Emery tried, failing to keep himself still.

"I don't care."

"Kinch, I kinda have a deadline—"

"And I don't care!" If Kinch could have slammed his hands down, he would have. "Why the fuck should I? You're making my replacement, aren't you?"

Ah.

"You heard that?" he asked quietly.

"I can't move." Kinch scowled again. "I'm not deaf. Of course I heard. That's why you've been avoiding me, isn't it? You don't want to feel guilty once they scrap me."

"They're not going to scrap you," Emery said hesitantly. He wasn't sure if that was true or not, but he wasn't going to just sit by and wait and see. "And I'm not making your replacement."

"If you're going to lie to me, you can just leave."

Emery left, but not because he was lying. When Kinch got like this, he was stubborn, and it was hard for him to be able to have a conversation without him making Emery feel stupid, and Emery generally felt stupid enough that he didn't like it when Kinch added on to that.

Kinch was the smart one—smart, elegant, and resourceful. Emery was just a dumb hunk of metal. And he knew Kinch didn't mean it. He was kinder than he put out, and he was a good person to talk to despite his pessimism, but there were bad days, and there was only Emery for him to take his anger out on. So instead of bothering to make it worse, Emery picked up his project and dumped it right on top of Kinch's, pinning the beginnings of a dress shirt to the workbench and underneath the metal.

"You oaf! What do you think you're doing?!" Kinch's head jerked up to meet him, golden eyes dully staring up at him. His movements were never smooth, not like Emery's. Fabric and metal did not move the same way. What had made Emery had taken care in his design, ensured he could move smoothly and work efficiently. Emery had many joints and could move as he pleased, work as precisely as he pleased. He could run and jump and pick things up without hassle. He could hold tools and craft and do his job. What had made Kinch…

Kinch moved as if someone were controlling him, as if there were someone invisible holding his arms and guiding them around. There was no way for him to move smoothly. He had no joints to speak of; he was the same shape as Emery but nowhere near as close in construction. Two arms, two legs, a torso, and a head. But metal was sturdy, and linens were…not so. They tore easily, and even now Emery could see stitches along his fingers, his hands, where he'd ripped flowery cloth apart from not being careful, the navy-blue threads standing out against the rest of him.

Kinch was fabric and stuffed with cotton packed too tightly. There was no support in any part of his body. It was a miracle he could move at all.

Emery stared down at Kinch, at the furious look on his face.

Kinch was still saying things to him, still yelling at him for getting in his way when he knew that Kinch couldn't clear his workspace by himself, but Emery was not listening.

"I made this for you," he told the fabric being, plainly so, not a hint of anger in his tone. Emery wasn't angry at him, could not be angry with him. He'd be angry too if he was confined to the same chair every day and had to rely on others to move him, no agency of his own. "It's a gift."

Kinch shut his mouth. Perhaps if he were made of something less soft, Emery would have heard the click of his jaw. He dropped his head, messily untangled himself from his sewing work—it had to be wrapped around his fingers just so to keep it from slipping out of his grasp; the needle pricked through the tip of his finger—and ran his hand along the gauntlets. They weren't proper gauntlets, most certainly not made for fighting, but Emery had yet to come up with a better name for them. They were much more delicate than weapons, but still just as sturdy. It was meant to be used for something much more precise than fighting, much softer.

"I'm sorry I didn't have them finished sooner."

Kinch's hands jerked to try the gauntlets on.

"Do you need help?" Emery did not move toward him. He wasn't sure if Kinch had realized what exactly this creation was meant to do, his partner oddly quiet as he tried to fit the metal over his fingers.

"I suppose," he answered dryly, trying not to look too excited.

Emery gently guided his partner's hands into the device. The gloves fit around his hands, clasping around his wrist and where his joints were meant to be. There wasn't any heft to them, meant to be light in their construction. The supports rested on his palms and on the undersides of his fingers. Emery had designed them so that they wouldn't pinch Kinch's fabric, wouldn't tear at him. He secured all the clasps and made sure they wouldn't come loose, making sure they were all the right size and wouldn't slip, feeling the metal coils inside him go slack when he realized they fit quite well, almost perfect. He checked things over once, twice, three times, then turned them on. Kinch watched with intrigue as it lit up, watched his own fingers twitch, gasping softly. He experimentally moved his fingers, and when they moved without issue, he wiggled them with delight, his face breaking into a wide smile that Emery had never seen on him before. The most he'd ever gotten out of Kinch was a smirk or a half-grin. His hands curled into fists, and then he opened them again, watching in complete awe. He picked up a swatch of fabric from his desk, marveling at himself.

"I have more pieces," Emery said, awkwardly shifting his stance, his heavy gait making scuffs on the tile floor.

Kinch looked up at him, mouth agape. "You do?"

"Elbows, knees," he explained with a flourish of his hand, gears clinking in time.

"Can I see them?"

Emery gathered up the rest of the pieces, Kinch still stuck in his chair but not for longer, listening in rapt attention as his partner explained each piece in turn, standing so that Kinch could see.

"Could you help me?" he asked once Emery was done, with all the same wonder and intrigue as a prototype.

Emery was just as careful with these pieces as he had with the gauntlets, snapping the clasps in place around Kinch's ankles and on his toes, above and below his knees and elbows, and around his thighs, his hands trying not to linger for modesty's sake, his body heating in slight embarrassment. He hoped Kinch was so infatuated with the devices that he wouldn't notice the excess of steam pouring out from his vents.

"There's one more for your back," he said once he was finished, handing off the last piece to Kinch. "One part to go around your neck and one to go around your waist."

He covered his eyes as Kinch hiked up the hem of his dress without shame or hesitation, peaking once he heard the clasp snap into place, the brace snaking up his back, hidden underneath bright yellow. The final clasp was shut, and Emery flipped all the switches.

Emery watched him stand on his own, wobbly and unsure of himself but smiling.

"I can work," Kinch whispered to himself. "I can—"

Emery caught him before he could hit the floor, and Kinch laughed.

"Perhaps I need a cane or a walker." He stood, brushing Emery off of him. "Wait, I—"

Kinch took the fabric still in his fist, tying his yarn brown hair up and out of his face. He stumbled his way to Emery's part of the workshop, rifling through the drawers with his newfound movement. He began pulling bits and bobs out of places, working them over in his hands, Emery watching him silently. He looked so proper on this side of the shop, among scraps of metal. It took him a few tries to be able to grasp the tools properly, to get a hang of his newfound movement, but he seemed to be a fast learner.

"I don't know what to do!" Kinch laughed as he spun Emery's chair around. Why did it look like he fit there? Why did it look like this had always been his side of the room? Why could Emery not recognize it as his own? "I want to make—I want to make *everything.* Is that possible?"

"I take it you like my gift." It wasn't even a question. No contest. Anyone could have seen how happy he looked.

"You built me an exoskeleton," Kinch said in disbelief, still staring down at his hands, wiggling his fingers again. "I love it!"

"Ah, so that's the word," Emery mused to himself, smiling sadly. "*Exoskeleton.* That's a good word. I wouldn't have thought of that."

Kinch's smile fell. "What's wrong? Your invention works, doesn't it?"

It did. "It works perfectly."

"I suppose I'll need some practice. You'll have to teach me how to use the tools."

Emery suddenly found it hard to speak. "You already know, don't you?"

"Well, yes, in theory," he shrugged. "But it would be nice to have some help. I can't write either. And I'm not sure about the whole walking thing. More mobility aids might be necessary. I can count on you for that, right, partner?"

"I...I'm not sure I'll be here for much longer."

"What?" Kinch's hand was on his shoulder, clamping down. Kinch was nearly the same height as him. Huh. Strange. He'd never noticed. "They're transferring you? Since when?"

"I'm not being transferred." He took Kinch's hand off his shoulder.

"You're quitting?!" His bottom lip began to tremble. "You can't quit! We have work to do! I'm finally able to work with you, and *you're leaving?"*

Emery couldn't meet his eyes. They were the only parts of Kinch that were made of metal. Pure, solid gold—polished to perfection. Kinch always hated them. Emery thought they were pretty.

"I'm not needed anymore."

Kinch grabbed his face and pulled him downward so that he was looking Emery right in the eyes. "What the hell are you talking about?"

"I disobeyed." Emery took a step back, moving around Kinch to put his tools back. "I *was* supposed to be making your replacement. I didn't."

"They'll look past it once they see this." Kinch held out his hands. "Look at this—this is better than a replacement—"

"You don't get it. Everything I made was *your* idea," he sneered. "That's how this all went. You think of it, I make it; everyone believes I'm smart and that I'm worth something because they don't think you're capable of doing anything beyond sewing."

His hand rested on the shelf above him, pausing. The vents in his back let out a burst of steam. "You can work now. You can make your own ideas without my help. Higher-ups would find it better to train you and scrap me than keep us both around. All I'm good at is making things you tell me to. You can think up these amazing things, and now you can make them yourself. Out of the two of us, you have a future. I don't."

Kinch didn't respond. Emery kept putting his tools away.

"It's not a race," Kinch whispered after a while. "It's not a game. I'm not measuring my worth against you—"

"We're not, but they are, and an inventor that can't actually invent isn't worth what he's made of. In their eyes, I'm better off scrap."

He heard Kinch muddle his way toward him, and he did something unexpected.

Kinch wrapped his arms around his waist, hugging him from behind. "I'm not going to let them scrap you."

"Kinch—"

"You're my partner, Em, even if I don't act like it sometimes. I'm sorry."

"You don't need a partner," he argued. "You're better off without me."

Kinch pulled away from him, smacking him in the back of the head.

"Hey! Don't dent me!" Emery spun to look at him.

"I'm full of cotton—I can't dent you if I tried!" Kinch hissed; each word punctuated with a finger jabbing him in the chest. "You don't get to make decisions for me! No one does! You're my partner, whether you like it or not.

Understand? You're important. You made me this exoskeleton even though you thought you'd get scrapped for it. *You* made it, not me. And even if I did help you—so what?! We're partners! We're supposed to work together, and I can't do this without you."

"You can find anyone to teach you to write and to work," Emery said coldly.

"You're missing the point!" Kinch grabbed him by the shoulders and started shaking him. "I don't want to work with anyone else or by myself. I want you!"

"Why?"

"Because you're my friend." Kinch let him go, golden eyes looking sheepishly at the floor. "I know I don't act like it, and I really am sorry. You're brilliant, really. You're not stupid, even if you think you are, and you're not worthless. Look at me. Look what you've made. You're—you're the only one who doesn't look at me like I'm hopeless, and you've gone through all this trouble to help me. I've always wanted to be an inventor, and you're the only one I've felt comfortable trusting with that. I was made for sitting still and being pretty. I was made to be looked at, not for working, but all I wanted to do was make things like you. You never told me it was a stupid idea, never told me I should give up. You helped me bring my inventions to life, and there's no way I could ever thank you enough for that. And I'm not good at telling people those things, and I think I'm messing this up because I keep talking about me, but I care about you even if I don't show it. I don't want you to be scrapped; I don't want you to relocate or quit—I want you here, with me."

Emery felt something inside him lurch, felt a particularly large set of gears come to a halt for an extended period of time. When they restarted, he managed to speak again.

"Careful now. You're starting to sound like you actually tolerate me."

Kinch huffed, but he couldn't wipe the smile off his face. "Obviously not, idiot...but you are staying, right? Because I don't think I can stand much longer."

As he said that, he collapsed into Emery's arms.

"Are you alright?"

"Standing is quite exhausting. I don't know how you do it," he grunted, steadying himself as he rested against his partner, looking up at him. The thread that patched an old tear on his left cheek looked a little worn. Kinch caught him staring. "She liked to pinch my cheeks, my creator. Didn't care that it tore me, that *she* tore me. Unavoidable. She was...rough edges. Always told me how beautiful I was. Always dressing me up and decorating me, parading me around like an ornament. Always introduced me as *hers* too. She just had to let everyone know that she made me, and they'd always say how pretty I was. I hated it. Being *just pretty*."

"I think you're beautiful," Emery blurted, then looked away, aware that Kinch was still in his arms like some sort of fainting maiden. *Not the time.* "I, uh, like your flowers; I mean, um—"

"You're also insufferable," Kinch said, poking him in the nose. "But at least you're sincere. I'm pretty sure I was made to fish for compliments."

"You were made to invent. Why else would you be so smart?"

Kinch reached up and patted him on the cheek. "Just keep complimenting me like that. You...*are* staying, right?"

"Ask me nicely."

"Please?" Golden eyes looked up at him, pleading. "Please stay?"

Not fair, not fair, not fair—

"Well," Emery said, as if he were still considering it. "I would like to learn how to sew. Someone has to make sure you don't hurt yourself tripping all over the place. Do you want to start with a cane or a walker?"

"Can we make both? Oh! And I'll need my own workbench! And my own tools! I can't wait!"

Emery really wished he could smile.

Angler

There *is* a way to tell if a drowning thing is dead yet or not.

In darkness, the only way to tell is to feel and to listen. There is the heartbeat, first and foremost, and keen ears are able to detect that easily, even if it is eerily silent. There is heat in a still-living body—this far deep, everything was cold, frigid. A dead thing, by the time its carcass sank this far down, wouldn't have been warm, chilled by the ice-cold waters. Or, well, he supposed it was cold to the things from above. Either way, it was strange to find one of them this deep that was still alive. Cold, but not as cold as dead meat, heart beating although very, *very* quiet and unsteady. Definitely not breathing. Not even a single bubble of air came past its lips. But it wasn't dead.

Yet.

There was something morally ambiguous about this situation. Would it be worth it to kill the already dying creature, or should he wait until its heart stopped completely to render the flesh from its bones and start to eat? It would die either way, but would he be disheartened if it died by his own hands? He was already accustomed to eating creatures like this—the things with spindly arms like his and a face like his and an upper body like his. He had no qualms about killing to satisfy his hunger, but there was something else about the concept of killing a creature that was similar to his stature, something that wasn't too detrimental, but it made him pause either way.

They were usually dead by the time they got this far down, but this one, surprisingly, was not.

Should I?

He reached out toward the thing. He knew its shape by touch, very much like his, except its tail was cleaved into halves, poor thing. All of them were like that, mutilated in the same manner. It had no spikes or barbs, with soft skin instead of the rough leather like his, an absence of scales, flat teeth, and hands that were not clawed and not webbed. The top of its head was soft, like plant life but not quite, and it had two round things above its nose. Round, squishy things that burst when he bit them.

But he didn't eat this one yet, still considering if he should or if he should wait.

He always wondered where they came from, why they were always dead when he found them—all except for this one, which was continuously fading by the second. But he figured the lack of gills was to blame, his clawed hands running over the skin of its neck in amazement. They always dropped, like stones, always came from above. And it bothered him, of course, but he never thought too hard about it when these dead things gave him a low-effort meal. The ones above him, the ones that don't need spikes or sharp teeth and have those same bulbs in the center of their faces—*eyes,* he remembered—say that there is something else above the water, that it's like living in a bubble, and that those things breathe *air.*

He didn't get to ask anything else. They swam away from him. They didn't like it when he went farther up. They didn't eat these sinking creatures. They weren't like him, much too soft. They didn't eat meat, turned their noses up at it, and they died easily. They were closer to him than this thing, however, with their hard flippers and tough plating on their backs. Those ones, he never got to examine them too closely, too far away for him to touch, but occasionally he'd find a dead one and, well, food is food is food.

He patted down the thing in his grasp, the dying one with no breaths left to give. He prodded at its face, at its body. Felt the peeling of something that seemed to float away from its body, not quite attached. Perhaps it was shedding. He never did like the way that softer skin tasted, so good on it for learning how to shed. He marveled at how this thing—definitely an adult by its size but with a much shorter, ripped tail than his—fought with no claws or fangs or barbs. These things weren't even poisonous! He'd never taken the time to consider these things before. He didn't know why he was so interested now.

And suddenly he wasn't so hungry, so much as curious.

If this thing breathes air…

He pressed his mouth to the thing, exhaling deeply. Without gills, this thing wouldn't breathe like him. Mouths made bubbles, and bubbles were full of air, so if it breathed air, he'd just make bubbles go into it. He was grasping at a solution that didn't seem very optimistic, but it was the only one he had.

He felt the thing twitch in his arms, but it didn't stir. It was such a warm thing compared to him, and he wanted to nuzzle it closer, but that was not important right now. Its heartbeat picked up slightly as it shivered. It would still die if it stayed down here. It had to go higher, back where it came from.

Could *he* go up higher? Could he get to the above-water place, survive there?

He wasn't sure, carefully taking his mouth away from the thing, careful not to bite at its lips. The higher he went, the harder it was to get his bearings. There was just too much to focus on up high.

But—

He swam upward, going slowly, careful to make sure the thing in his arms could breathe, that it had enough air, stopping every so often to ensure it was still alive.

His face began to sting the higher he went. This was usually where he stopped, where he went back down to the depths to make this feeling—this sting, this hurt, this pain—stop. He kept going. He accidentally bit the thing, once, his teeth scraping against its face, and its blood smelled so good, *so tempting,* but he ignored his growling stomach and pressed on.

He wanted to know what the above was like, wanted to ask this thing why it had no claws or gills.

He nearly let the thing go, let it sink, when his face split open above the nose, the pain becoming unbearable. He scrunched up his face, trying so hard to make it stop. It hurt too much, so much that he wanted to cry out, to start wailing, but he had to get this thing upwards, into the air.

Air was sharp and cold, much colder than the bottom of the sea, and it cut into his skin, rough and horrid and unfamiliar.

He whimpered as he felt it for the first time, once more pressing his mouth to the creature in his arms, trying to force the water out of it. It made a wretched noise, bulbs—eyes—fluttering open, and he realized that he could…what was the word? It wasn't just touch anymore, the thing in front of him. In front of him, eyes trained on him, specifically the bulb protruding from his head, the glowing one that lured prey in. It was loud in his eyes. It was so loud and it stung and it hurt and he didn't know how to make it stop.

"Holy crap."

He didn't like this, didn't like eyes trained on him, didn't like how *bright* everything was, how much it hurt him. He let the thing go and dove back down.

"Hey—wait!"

He looked up at the thing—apparently, it could swim after all, even with its broken tail. He flung himself back into the depths, remembering that creature, and how it looked.

That was a word, right? *Looked?*

Back in the darkness, he pressed the palm of his hand to a newly formed eye, gently rubbing at it. It seemed like they were here to stay.

In the pitch-black depths, it was just him and the glowing ball of light.

Light of the Divine

It was routine by now. Sweep the floor around the altar. Dust it. Lay out the appropriate clothes and coverings, then the offerings. Light the candles. Say your prayers, clasp your hands, and bow low. *Sweep, dust, lay, light, pray, clasp, bow. Sweep, dust, lay, light, pray, clasp, bow. Sweep, dust, lay, light, pray, clasp, bow.* It was a calming mantra and a good way to remember the chores. Not that their worship was considered a chore, but the task of upkeep was similar to that of keeping house. His mother had always scolded him for comparing it to washing his laundry or cooking dinner, but those were semantics. They were chores, plain and simple.

Nox understood that being caretakers of an altar was an important task and that families assigned to such holy work were privileged in a way that others were not. He had faith, and like his mother, it would not falter. However, it was sometimes hard to consider yourself lucky when the entity you were meant to serve did not give you the courtesy of accepting your offerings. Nox didn't take offense to it personally, because apparently whatever being that was meant to accept their offerings did not find offense with them. They just…didn't bother to show up. Hadn't since the altars were first constructed, if the others were to be believed, the name of the deity long forgotten. His family still kept up their duties. It was still sacred, still their responsibility. It didn't matter if people would whisper when they had their backs turned, calling them disgraceful. It didn't matter if someone showed up—it was work that needed to be done.

Nox tied off the bundles of herbs he was holding and set them among the rest. That was the last of them. He could feel eyes on the back of his neck, but he had gotten used to them, having been stared at since he was small. An altar was still an altar, and it still needed to be served, even if its deity did not claim it as such. When he was younger, he had dreams of the angel they served coming to claim their gifts, praising him for doing such a good job. He no longer dreamed of such delusions now, but that did not stop him from doing his job. His mother was getting on in years, and it was harder for her to make it across town to tend to this sacred place, so he made the weekly journey alone.

Occasionally, his mother would make her way over regardless of how much he protested—"I can still pray, *sabiħ*. Rest is for dead people."—and Nox would at least have company during the day. She was now sitting in the pew closest to their altar, watching him and giving him pointers, even though he'd been doing this for years, both with her help and without. He liked the work, but sometimes he had to wonder if there was an angel for them. No one knew their name or what they granted. Who was to say their family had ever been assigned to an actual angel at all?

His mother would have killed him if he ever uttered his suspicions out loud, and it wasn't often that he got those thoughts, but it was nice to believe that it wasn't their fault, that their family was not cursed was not forsaken, as others believed.

Perhaps it would have been better if he had been satisfied with forsaken.

The storm that swept through the temple made the hairs on his arms stand on end. The darkened clouds of broiling thunder filled the room, blotting out the sunlight pouring in from the outside, disembodied whispers chittering away. The crowd scrambled to find shelter, the angels of the other alters standing to attention as they eyed the commotion, heading, seemingly, straight for Nox and his mother.

Nox's first thought was, *I swear to fuck if I have to bundle all those herbs again*—and he was abruptly caught off-guard as the clouds dispersed, a young man standing at the foot of their alter, studying it intently.

To say he was bright was an understatement. The man shone as if he were a lighthouse on the darkened sea. He shone with gold, and yet his appearance, like the others, was marginally plain. Not a blemish on his pale skin, the beauty of something angelic crafted into a mimicry of a human form.

Nox suppressed a shudder when the angel, dressed in commoner's clothes unlike the rest of the pantheon, stared at him with equally golden eyes, their gaze lingering for a moment before turning back to the altar.

One could have heard a pin drop.

And then—

"Get the fuck out of here, Lucian!" Mikael, one of the more frequent angels, screeched into the tense silence.

"Yeah!" Another piped up. "No one wants you here, you bastard!"

The other angels began to jeer as well, with murmurs surfacing throughout the crowd of worshippers as they tried to make sense of what was happening. A flaming candle came soaring overhead, and Nox pushed his mother back as it landed at his feet, the roar of the other angels now deafening.

The angel with golden eyes—Lucian, so that was his name—scowled, a low growl forming in his throat, and the hall went silent. Nox felt something curl inside his gut. Something was wrong, something was horribly, terribly wrong. Why were they being looked at with such scorn? Why was this angel bringing this fury upon them? Why them? What had Nox and his mother done to deserve this? What had *Lucian* done?

This wasn't supposed to happen. Angels were meant to be divine, to be sacred, to be righteous. What was this?

Nox had a bad feeling about this.

"I am the same as you," Lucian addressed the crowd, his voice neither rising nor his tone becoming angry, but it caused them to still all the same. "I have every right to be here. Like you, I would like to partake in the festivities. You do not get to deny me the same privileges you wholeheartedly enjoy. I offer clarity to those who need it. I cast away the doubts of the mind and give one the volition necessary to pursue a future that they desire. You may approach me if you seek guidance direction."

Pompous jerk, Nox thought, holding his tongue as the congregation began to slowly approach, all curious at what this new being could offer them. He didn't like this; an ill feeling settling inside him. Why now? Why not show up for—supposedly—thousands of years, only to show up for no good reason? Nox didn't like this Lucian fellow; he didn't like the air of importance he had when he didn't even bother to speak with his caretakers. Years upon years of ignored offerings, his mother's pride, wasted, and this creature didn't even bother to give them the time of day. The very thing he claimed to come to the temple for, and this thing was above a simple *thank you.*

"You're not really going to see him?" Nox whispered under his breath as his best friend, Helen, passed by.

She shrugged. "I'd like to see what all the fuss is about. He can't be that great if all the other angels dislike him. I can at least say I know for sure. He's probably bullshit, anyway."

The angel smiled at her as she stepped forward. He placed his hands on either side of her face, cradling it gently. Helen's eyes sparked with gold, and Nox inhaled sharply. It looked like what he assumed lightning in a bottle would, a burning fire that looked like no other upon this earth. The glow of the angel's hands lit up her face, onlookers watching with bated breath to see what would happen. It was only a few moments before it all faded before the light dimmed. Helen took a deep breath as her eyes returned to normal. Lucian rested his hands on her shoulders reassuringly, and he smiled at her.

"What a lovely future." He sighed. "You're quite the dreamer."

"I—" Helen blushed. "I suppose."

"There now. You have an idea of what you wish to do with your life?"

"Yes. I believe I do."

She straightened herself, standing taller than she had been a moment ago, her eyes bright. Nox had seen her almost every day since he was born, but never had he seen her so unburdened, so peaceful. He watched her walk out of the temple, and when he could slip away from his mother, he followed, wondering what exactly she had seen, finding her by her cart, loading it up with supplies from nearby vendors that weren't preoccupied with worship. Within just a few minutes, her cart was nearly full to the brim.

"What're you doing?"

"I'm leaving. *Leaving* leaving." Helen stood up from where she was on the back of the cart, with a few people helping her load up her spoils. "I need to get out of this town and see the world. I'm not happy here. I mean, you've been a great friend, and this will always be my home, but I can't just let my life pass me by while I'm here being a farmhand. I want to go places. I never knew just how badly I wanted it until that angel showed me."

"What happened to being bullshit?"

"I was wrong." She hopped down from the cart, pulling him into a hug. "I'll write you, okay? I won't forget about you. You're still my best friend. I just…need some time away."

Nox sighed. Helen had talked about leaving before and about traveling, but she'd never considered it so seriously before. Nox couldn't argue that this was completely out of the blue. If this was what she wanted, he couldn't stop her. And while Nox didn't like the guy upon first impression, he was an angel. That meant his gifts, his powers, his guidance were all divine. He had to trust that Helen would be safe and that she would enjoy her new life.

He slipped back inside before his mother could notice his absence. Their altar was much more crowded than before; the entire thing nearly bathed in golden light as Lucian gave them all visions of a better life.

Harmless, in theory, but Nox still didn't like it. He still didn't trust the ethereal being, not when he had ignored their family for centuries and had strolled in here acting like he was owed. Nox also didn't like his mother being so openly accepting of all of this. Yes, it was something she took pride in, in being the altar's caretaker, but not once had this being granted them the decency to let them know that he was there at all. Even now, he still hadn't even said a word about their offerings, about all the work they'd gone through for him. Countless ancestors had done the same thing for blessings-knows-how-long. What would they say now if they saw such arrogance, knowing that they wasted their lives worshipping such a rude thing?

When the flow of worshippers died down later in the day, Lucian finally turned to Nox and his mother. "So, you two are my caretakers, yes?"

"Astraea," she greeted, pushing her son forward to present him, "and this is my boy, Noxell."

"Nox," he corrected, mumbling under his breath. He would only be as polite as he had to be and hoped he wouldn't come back a second time, leaving his mother to her delusions that this was a being that had merely blessed them with his presence.

"I don't mean to impose on the two of you, but I would require lodgings, just for tonight." He smiled at them, and

Nox didn't like the way it sat on his face, as if it were painted on rather than just *was*. "Your altar is very much appreciated, and I normally wouldn't ask this of caretakers such as yourselves, but I would be forever grateful."

Holy fuck, I hate this guy.

Nox stayed quiet as his mother began to fuss over their, apparently, new house guest. He stayed quiet while she talked about going home to prepare their house for Lucian. He stayed quiet as she told him that she would go home and do these things and that he would escort their guest when he was finished with the congregation.

And then he was left with the feeling of eyes staring at the back of his head.

"Why are you here?" Nox asked when he was sure his mother couldn't hear the crassness of his tone. "Why now? You had thousands of years to show up, thousands of years to answer my family—thousands of years of worship—and you ignored every single one of them."

"I don't want worship," Lucian said, shrugging.

"Then why did you bother showing up?"

"I find humans interesting. I want to see what they can do. I truly want to give people clarity. I wanted to share my gifts with them, so I broke my silence. If you were looking for some explanation about you being *special,* then I'm going to have to disappoint you."

"You don't have the right to do that, to string people along—"

"I didn't ask for that." Lucian's eyes gave him a once-over, as if he were deciding what to do to him, as if he wanted to hurt him. Nox did not back down. "I didn't ask for your family to spend years of letdown after letdown waiting for me. That is not my fault. I didn't ask for worship—I didn't ask for an altar. I am only here because it is such a large congregation, and I knew my colleagues would also be here."

The rest had gone now. It was just Lucian, and Nox had seen their disgust thrown at him, the way they sneered. He still didn't know why he was so hated so. Was it because he never showed up? Because he was *improper?* He supposed it wasn't the worst offense the angel could have committed, and he was still doing what he was meant to, offering to help people. He couldn't find fault in that, in the angel doing his duty to aid humanity, but he still hated the man's snobbery.

Nox bit his tongue as an older gentleman walked up to them.

"You offer guidance?"

"I suppose I do," Lucian answered.

The man nodded. "I have some regrets. I want to know if they were worth it."

Lucian took the man's face in his hands, and Nox watched again as they began to glow. This one was short, and when Lucian pulled away, he had a strange look on his face.

"Thank you," the man said as he came back to his senses.

"I do hope you make the right choice."

He grasped Lucian's hands, smiling. "Bless you."

Nox watched him go, watched Lucian's strange expression, wondering what it all meant, but he didn't have to wait too long as a shrill scream pierced the air.

Outside was a madhouse. Blood pooled on the stairs of the temple, and Nox watched in horror as a woman was pulled away from it, away from the man—the same man that Lucian had just given a vision to—wielding a bloodstained knife, lunging at her as he was restrained by the crowd. The woman scrambled to get back to the bloodied man, the body now wailing at the top of her lungs.

Nox didn't process much else. The knife was taken from the man, and he was taken away. A few people were kneeling next to the grieving woman, who was still on the red-painted steps, sobbing loudly as others moved to take the dead man away to prepare him for burial. All Nox could think of was the way the man had smiled at Lucian, at him, as if he'd been shown the secrets of the universe. The man had smiled when Lucian had shown him carnage, the act of taking another's life. He'd smiled when he'd been taken away, smiled as this woman cried out her grief for her dead husband.

"He chose wrong." Lucian sighed, quiet enough that Nox was the only one that heard him as he walked away from the scene, snapping the caretaker out of his stupor. Nox once more followed back into the temple, now empty.

"What the fuck did you do?"

Lucian was lighting the now-burned-out candles on the altar. "I didn't do anything."

"You showed him a vision, and he went out and killed someone! He would've killed that woman too if they hadn't stopped him!"

"So?" The angel turned toward him. "How is that my fault? I showed him what he wanted. What he did with that information was entirely his decision."

"You're not supposed to be like this."

"Then what am I supposed to be? You honestly thought I was righteous?"

"But you—you—" Nox swallowed, his words leaving him.

"I what?" Lucian tilted his head to the side, studying him curiously. "Shine brightly? Am painted with gold? Am one of many divine beauties? That's just how I am. You humans think in black and white, and it's exhausting. I came here because I was bored. I avoid altars and worshippers. I hate all of it, hate the idea that just because I am something else, I deserve something greater. I wanted to see what has changed after all these years, and nothing has. You all are still so *simple* that you can't see past all the bells and whistles that come with my powers. All your preconceived notions of what you think is right and good and just, and then you get mad when things aren't what you expected them to be."

"So inciting others to kill is good?"

"I never said that." He sighed. "You see me bathed in light, you see me as I am, and you think that because I am the way that I am, because I represent something as precious as wisdom, that automatically makes me something blessed. Wisdom is my guiding light, *clarity* is my guiding light—not purity, not goodness, and *certainly* not righteousness. You equate divinity with morality. You see me as, to be frank, angelic. And perhaps, with all the power I possess, I am, but I never said that I was pure, that I was holy. You humans prescribe that to me—*the others* prescribe that to me. But no, I'm not any of those things. I'm just me."

"You saw what that man was going to do," Nox spat. "You could have told someone. You could have stopped it. You're disgraceful."

"I won't deny that." Lucian took a step toward him, and on instinct, Nox stepped back.

"Keep your corruption away from me."

The angel sighed again. "You're still thinking in black and white. I do not corrupt, but I do not bless either."

Nox's dark eyes flicked over him.

"Like I said, I am wisdom. Enlightenment. I show people what they want and give them the clarity they desire. What I show them is not the certain future. It is *a* future, one that they want—and yes, that includes the violent ones. Whether they pursue it is up to them, not to me. I've just helped them decide what they want. I cleared their thoughts of doubt. I gave them a choice. That man chose to follow his violent desires. It wasn't set in stone that he would have killed anyone. He chose to resort to violence, to murder. Wisdom isn't just spouting off poetic nonsense about life and love. Wisdom is knowing oneself and knowing what one needs to do in life. It is knowing the consequences of your actions. It is also the gruesome truth, like the fact that any one of my cohorts would most likely raze this city if their offerings stopped, simply because they are that full of themselves."

"Would you?" Nox's voice shook, and there was a tremor in his voice as his lip began to wobble.

"My colleagues have convinced themselves that they are divine. I have no such delusions. I am simply not human. That does not make me any more important, it simply grants me a power that your kind does not possess—a power that is neither inherently good nor evil. They despise me because whatever violence I show causes them to lose their precious worshippers. I value life, but I also value the decision to choose, and I choose to give people clarity. I choose not to behave the same as them, and I see that I am a tool of this world, not a god. I have a job to do, and so do you. You are my caretaker, are you not?"

"I—" He faltered. To take care of the altar was his task, his duty, but could he do so *knowing* what Lucian was, what he brought, and what he left in his wake?

Did he have the stomach to worship something that could very well tear this world apart at its seams?

"Let me help you." Lucian took Nox's face in his hands, his eyes shimmering as they lit up like golden stars as his power worked its way to the altar boy. The human gasped, overwhelmed at the blinding heat and light that did not burn. He shook, trembled, grasping at something to hold onto, and then it was over.

"Now, do you know what you're going to do?"

"Didn't you see?" Nox asked, then realized he was still being held, shoving the angel away from him. "Don't touch me! Stop touching me! Get away!"

Lucian pursed his lips, trying to make himself look innocent, and it only made Nox want to punch that honest-to-gods *pout* off of the immortal being's face. "I thought you would have liked some privacy. You seem like the type to complain about that sort of thing."

"Stop patronizing me."

"Well?" the angel asked, raising an eyebrow. "What're you going to do?"

He still didn't like him. Not one bit.

Nox bowed. "I'm at your service."

"Don't grovel," Lucian ordered, but there was a sly smile on his face regardless. "I find it pathetic."

An Open Letter

Tell me how you really feel...

Jack was a simple boy. Scrawny, scared, most definitely could not hold up in a fight. Limbs too thin to have any sort of muscle behind them, but his mind was sharp enough to keep him on his toes. The boy, going on nineteen years of age based on what he had told me, was not a fighter but a healer, which I took to mean that he kept the fighters from dying. Meaning more trouble for me. Fighters, brawlers, adventurers, heroes—they were all too hot-headed for my tastes, too much to deal with. Their egos were larger than their weapons, and it was exhausting to deal with their business.

I do not have the patience for ████. *I think they meant "heroes."*

Idiots, all of them, but I suppose that is why they all came to The Library.

The building itself, from the outside at least, did not look like anything special—not that I had seen it or anything, but from what Jack had told me, it looked like a normal library, whatever that was supposed to mean. The inside, of course, was where all the fun happened.

Please do not be discouraged by the tedious horror story I am about to tell. It is necessary for context, *Really?* although I find it much too, how do you say, over the top? Anyway, this is how Jack tells the story. IT MOST CERTAINLY IS NOT!!!!

Deep in the bowels of an ancient city, within its library, there lies a most treacherous beast. It lurks within its den, hoping to catch those that have foolishly wandered in without preparation, its prey unsuspecting as it descends.

You should have become a poet.

Those that have managed to come out alive tell their brethren about the monster most foul that dwells within the city center, waiting for the sound of footsteps. Those that do not come back have the stains of blood marked upon the floor, their bones clattered into a heap in the deepest pit of its hell, freakishly white with the absence of flesh that has been disposed of in the foulest way, each bone scrubbed clean like an obsession. *You dramatic bitch.*

The creature itself does not have any stains on it. It is clean, meticulous—not a single drop of blood mars its wears. For all its intellect, *brag* its cunningness, it does not possess claws or fangs. It is ultimately the plainest thing you have ever seen, and that is how it draws you in. It makes you believe that no harm shall befall you and that you have every chance of slaying it if necessary and fleeing with your spoils. Any passer-by will tell you that the building is just that, a building, but the locals know better.

You're taking too long.

It is a dungeon, one not with traps designed to keep things out but one that was always meant to draw its food in.

See? Too much. YOU THINK???

Same here.

The Library is endless, as far as I can tell. Infinite knowledge stockpiled over centuries through various sources, all gathered in one convenient place. Anyone who conquers The Library shall conquer the world, as within these tomes were dangerous spells, rituals, and all sorts of things.

Which brings purpose to The Librarian.

STOP DOODLING ON MY MANUSCIPT, YOU FUCKING ASSHOLE!!!!!

The Librarian is the affectionate name for the creature that lives within The Library, the aforementioned monster that kills whoever takes *(EXCEPT ME!!!)* a step within its domain. It makes sense if you think about it. Power, glory, fame, blah blah blah—not too good if it falls into the wrong hands, so what better way to deal with it than to have everyone who goes after it eaten and die a very painful death? Ingenious, if you ask me, as it deals with both the intruders, and not a single coin would be spent on feeding the thing. I wish I could shake the hand of whoever thought it up, but then again, I probably ate him too. *Why though?*

No one is sure what The Librarian is or where it came from, least of all me, but that is inconsequential to this story. This story is about my friend Jackwise. The only being, human or other, to step foot inside and make it out in one piece, without a single scar or scrape about him.

I find him fascinating. *Awwwww.* Shut up.

Some people come out of The Library, very few, in fact, but they are missing quite a few things when they come back out—arms, legs, eyes. You know, the essentials. Even if one is not tempted by the glory of all that untapped knowledge, adventurers come in droves, hoping to take something from its stores. It is still an archive of information, and sometimes one needs the right book to learn how to defeat an evil lich king, banish a dragon, or what have you. So, people risk their lives not only for conquest but also because they have their own things going on and need a solution. The Library is the very last resort for those righteous types. I've heard they draw lots to see who goes in, which is a bit pathetic if you consider what might happen if that group needs to come back again for whatever reason.

Jackwise informs me while writing this that the first time he came into The Library, he volunteered.

The kid was fourteen! I wasn't going to let him die!

Age is simply a number.

You're terrible...

Why anyone would sacrifice their life for another is beyond me.

Anyways, when I met him, he was in The Library, on the ~~third~~ *Fourth* floor if I remember correctly. A thing about this particular library is that the floors are sub-terranean. Only the main floor, the entrance, is above ground. All other floors—however many there are—*I've counted 47 so far*—are underground. The only way to go is down. *Hush, you.*

So, ~~three~~ *FOUR!!!!* floors down, I met this <u>unassuming</u> *I prefer handsome* young boy.

The first time I saw him, I looked like a human girl.

<u>*THAT WAS YOU?!*</u>

He was a bit smaller than he was now, much different from the other fighters I'd come in The Library. Like I'd said at the beginning of the chronicle, Jack is a spindly thing—that hadn't changed in the years I've known him. He is not a fighter but a healer and is not equipped to handle any the dangers The Library possesses—if not The Librarian, then the other adventurers who were looking for others to pick off rather than venture deeper and incur the wrath of the beast.

Still waiting for my growth spurt...
I have noodle arms

He had been hiding under a desk, which had been a bit overturned from the thick roots that ran across this specific floor. There was a tree growing out of one of the walls—how it came to be three stories underground, I will never know. Its roots made this floor an obstacle course for adventurers, so it was smart for Jack to hide rather than run with this floor plan. This particular desk that Jack was hiding under was a favored spot among the adventurers that came this way, as evidenced by the large, dried bloodstain underneath him.

Tree is very good for climbing

Gross! Maybe people wouldn't try to kill you if you cleaned up a little.

For Jack, the place would have given him cover, perhaps from others passing by. It was a smart hiding place, all things considered.

Well, it would have been smarter to hide and not be found, but I'm good at finding things.

Fuck off

I will not lie—I liked scaring him. I dropped on top of the desk, head hanging off the side as I stared at him. He was lying on his side, knees pressed up to his chest. The leatherbound book in his possession was held tightly in his arms, being shielded by his limbs.

Of course, I felt the need to toy with him since I hadn't seen him before, so I crawled under the desk next to him. He didn't make a single sound, but he did jolt slightly at the contact as my shoulder bumped into his. I could hear his heart racing and smell the fear wafting off of his as he sat there, frozen.

He was terrified.

You scare me.

I take that as a compliment.

"What book is that?" I asked him because I was curious about the inventory. *← Highly recommend!*

"<u>Abbathicus' Book of Dragons</u>," he told me, keeping his voice low.

It was a good book, probably one of the better ones on both dragon caretaking and how to slay them (if it came to that).

There was a minute before he decided that the cost was clear, wiggling himself out from his hiding spot, then walked toward the eastern side of the building.

"Shuffle" maybe.

"Where are you going?" I had asked, pointing in the other direction. "The exit is that way."

"I'm putting this back where I found it."

His response baffled me. To this day, I still don't understand it. He was holding such a valuable book in his hands, worth enough that he would be set for the rest of his short human life, and he was returning it without much consideration. I was so stunned that I just stood there, watching him go reshelve the book, exactly where it was meant to be, no tears, no rips, each page immaculate.

→ You can say that again.

I WILL EAT YOU ALL YOU DO IS EAT!!!

I am not one for emotion, dear reader, but I felt…something. Confusion, surely, but there was something else as well. I later identified this as curiosity. Books do not come back to The Library if the odd one manages to be swindled away, and if they do, they come back with pages missing, burned, ripped, eaten, poisoned, cursed, what have you. I have had one come back that was growing moss between its pages, and I assure you it was not meant to do that.

(I will admit it was tasty, despite the stomach-ache I incurred later.)

STOP EATING MOSS!!!!!!!! IT'S NOT GOOD FOR YOU!!!!!!!

Still does♥...   I Do What I Want

This boy puzzled me so much, and I was so perplexed by him that I'd completely forgotten to disembowel him. I was upset at that revelation, but I was also much more preoccupied with the boy who'd said he had to return the book.

Meaning that he had been here before and stolen the book away, and I hadn't even noticed his presence. It is not often that I am outsmarted, so it does not so much anger me then it does impress me.

IS THAT A COMPLIMENT I SEE???

Don't let it go to your head. It's already too big.

You're like ten times my size, you ass!

You annoy me. Constantly.

I usually do end up pulling their joints from their sockets, breaking their bones and turning them into mincemeat once they get cocky and come back a second time, so there is no point in becoming furious when I will end up with food in the end. But this boy had already outsmarted me once and had the gall to distract me the second time around, so I felt particularly cheated out of a free meal.

Awww, you do love me!

I kept thinking about the boy, because not only did he bring back one of my books, but he also didn't even spare a second glance at me, not once considering that I might be dangerous or that I was attempting to steal his prize. Not once did he raise his sword or move to defend himself. He left himself wide open in front of someone he did not know, despite the terror he'd been experiencing.

The next time we met, I decided to change my shape. I wanted to provoke the boy—I wanted to see him fight, though I suppose no matter his prowess, I would be the victor. How long it would take for him to die would depend on how much of a show I wanted it to be. I will admit that I like playing with my food.

I made myself resemble that of an orc—a great, big beast of a thing with a hell of a temper. Surely, you know what an orc is? I haven't seen one in person, only in pictures, but I was sure it was an accurate representation. Orcs are large, orcs have large teeth, and orcs like to break things—particularly bones. My fragile intruder was sure to be spooked by my appearance and draw his sword and fight, and I would have the satisfaction of dealing with another pest.

I actually know an orc that is very polite. Also a very good baker.

48

Do you want to know what this pesky brat did?
He hid from me!!!!
He hid!!!

Again, I'm small.

~~Of all the~~
~~Horrid little bastard~~ ←
~~Fucking gods above~~ ←
~~That is the greatest insult I have ever~~

I'd like to know what the fresh fuck happened here

I apologize for my uncertainty of what to write next, because while Jack and I have since become friends, are on quite amicable terms, and I have grown quite fond of him, his actions upon this meeting make me terribly angry, but since then I have eaten and have calmed down.

Jackwise is being persistent in asking that I let him edit this once I am done writing. I do not think that course of action is wise, pun not intended, because my friend is quite the idiot in the sense that he has no filter and no, it is not important I write down what I eat I know you're reading over my shoulder, you little shit, stop it.

WHAT DID I DO?!?!

Please pardon that last part. I deeply apologize for getting off track. He is incredibly nosy, and I hate him.

You love me and you're no fun. Die.

The reason I find it infuriating that Jack was non-confrontational is that, as I've said, I like dinner and a show. If you're hunting something for sport, it is much more fun if your prey runs. There is no fun in idle prey, and I had been looking forward to watching this particular specimen run like a fox with hounds set upon it.

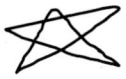

Is that the right phrase, Jackass?
Yeah, but don't call me that!

You'll see once we get outside.

Why stars?

I was quite miffed, lumbering around, pretending I could not spot him, hoping that maybe he would get scared and take his chances in fleeing, but no! He hid inside one of the floating wardrobes (located on the seventh floor, though I have no idea why all that furniture floats, and I despise it as it makes it harder to reach intruders, though I do get to them eventually. Tendrils are quite useful appendages).

I kept stalking about, hoping that maybe he'd show himself, but I've learned that Jack is incredibly patient, aggravatingly so.

He hid in that cupboard for four hours.

That was not fun. I had to pee so bad!

Disgusting...

I had not left the room, walking up and down the rows of shelves, pretending to look for something. About halfway through that fourth hour, I gave up and called out to him.

"Why are you still hiding? Aren't you tired and sore?"

I didn't expect him to answer, but he did, which was polite of him.

"Because once I leave," came the muffled reply, "you're going to fight me."

<u>Which was true, I'll give him that.</u>

You're why I have trust issues.

"If I promise I won't, will you come out?"

At this point, I was much more curious as to his behavior than I was hungry, and I supposed the elf I'd eaten earlier that day had a hand in that (the bastard had stabbed me in the thigh!).

ALL YOU DO IS TALK ABOUT FOOD!!!

It took a bit of fussing, but Jack came tumbling out of the cabinet, landing ungracefully on his ass. I was surprised he actually agreed to come out of hiding. He had another book in his possession—<u>Lilith's Introductory Almanac to Medicinal Herbs and Plants.</u> That wasn't a book meant to help on epic quests—I mean, when was the last time you heard of someone saving the world with flowers? Never, but I did not care about his choice in literature at the moment. I want to know why he wasn't going to draw his sword, which sat in its sheath, looking more like a decoration than anything of proper use.

Also recommended!

"You don't want a duel?" he asked me warily, and I set down the axe I had taken from one of the many intruders to complete my disguise.

"I want to talk. I've seen you here before. I want to know why you didn't try to fight your way past me. Did you think you would lose?"

He shrugged. "I just don't want to fight. I don't like it. I'm a healer, and I took an oath to do no harm."

"But you carry a sword—"

"That's not mine. My party gave it to me because they said I needed it. I haven't drawn it."

"Not even once?" I asked.

"Not even once."

Still haven't used it and fucking proud of it!

I began to pester him, of course, because no one else was in my den at the time (no one alive anyways). I asked him my questions about giving and taking books, on why he insisted on returning them when many, many people would kill for books like the ones he took—apparently quite often, and I hadn't noticed at all!

CAT??? Jack told me his methods. There was an opening on the roof from the outside that I had never seen. Each time he came here, he slipped inside, and while I was focused on the morons coming through the front door and descending the proper way, he would sneak by, taking one book each time not to arouse suspicion. He wasn't loud, nor brash, so he hid not to hide from me but from others like him that were foolish enough to try and attack me head-on, to make their presence known on purpose.

I'm skinny enough to fit. Not as fun as it sounds.

I'll take it!   <u>Jack is…smart in some ways that I must give him credit.</u> I am so preoccupied with the violent ones that the boy even had time to do his research! Each time he snuck into my lair, he would only take books with solutions to various quests, provided that the book would remain intact once whatever spell or ritual was complete.

Those poor books…

A lot of magic rituals involve burning pages or magic books turning to ask, and that angers me so. Adventurers that come to this library for tomes do not care what happens to the books, to the precious knowledge as long as they finish their quests and they get paid.

I asked him, if he was so successful, why he bothered returning them? Why not keep them for his own collection, or sell them?

He smiled at me and said, "Isn't that what a library is for? Borrowing?"

I told him of my true nature then and there. He laughed because I do have a reputation as a bloodthirsty monster, and I suppose that bloodthirsty monsters are not supposed to have manners. Regardless, I told him to keep the herbology book since it was helpful for his field of practice. He laughed even harder.

When he came back to return it, I gave him a good scare in return. I think he nearly soiled himself! *You're quite mean to me sometimes...*

I often wonder, dear reader, what would have happened to me had things gone differently that day. What would have happened if Jack had decided to break his oath to finally draw his sword? What if I had gotten hungry and had simply decided to eat him like I had originally planned? I suppose I would still be within The Library, going about my business as usual.

You might be wondering, "Why on earth would a being like you befriend a human?"

♥ *Because I'm adorable!* ♥

Because you're chewy. *SHAME ON YOU!*

Jack takes care of my books. I decided I would take care of Jack.

I like Jack. He is a good friend. I don't need any other reason than that.

Each time Jack came into my lair, I would let him go about as he always had. If any intruders tried to fight him, I would make short work of them. He told me about the outside world, of things I hadn't read in books—the world does change, after all. I let him freely explore The Library, wandering for days on end to be able to learn its secrets. He'd given up on traveling the outside world; the people he had been traveling with had proven to be just as vile as the ones I dealt with on a daily basis, and he had grown tired of their company. I still do not understand how he puts up with me, with my choice of food and messy eating habits, shall we say, but loyal Jack has remained my only friend.

I don't fault you for eating. You have to, to stay alive. Though you are a shameful glutton.

The point of all this blather, you ask?

I am The Librarian. I am the keeper of this knowledge, its guardian. Of course I would want to document a moment such as this, the making of my first and only friend, and what better way to do it than to write it in my own words?

Jackwise was the only person who has survived my wrath, and he has done so not <u>in spite</u> of never raising his weapon to me but <u>because</u> he chose an option that did not include violence. Make of that what you will, but I know for a fact that you people will misinterpret it and resort to trickery regardless. My friendship with him persists not because he tamed me or any similar nonsense, but because he was kind and because he was pacifist. Knowledge is granted to those with patience and virtue, not to those who seek glory or strength. I want you, dear reader, to know that it is because of this kindness, this friendship, that I will perhaps one day be able to achieve my dreams.

So, to whom it may concern, I, The Librarian, Beast of the Deep, have within my custody Jackwise No-Last-Name and have had him within said custody for the past few years. But what happened to Jack is not why you are reading this. This introduction, penned by my hand, is an explanation as to why I have left The Library. It will be the first installment of our research together, both of my den, The Library itself, in hopes that more can be learned about it and perhaps find a way to temporarily relieve myself from its walls. I cannot leave this place unguarded, but I wish to see the world. I wish it could have been Jack because he was so eager to explore this place, but his unwillingness to fight is not ideal if the knowledge is to remain within its walls. My replacement will have to be someone as powerful as me and willing. Finding them would be no easy task, but I have nothing but knowledge at my disposal. So, congratulations, for you are my worthy successor.

I'll keep them safe on the outside. Be good to this place – it is our home.

I wish I could name you, whoever you are, but as of writing this, I have not met you yet. All my life, millennia of it, has been spent reading about the outside, and I have been unable to experience it for myself. By exploring my den, the two of us wish to both document this place and hopefully find a way for me to be able to leave, to find someone to replace me—and if I do, the solution will be somewhere in these pages for when you decide to leave as well, in turn passing these writings, as well as your own, to your replacement.

If you are reading this, whether because I have given it to you or you have found it shelved away with the other resources I have left for you, then you know that this is meant to be a guide for you to learn how to take up my mantle. Perhaps I have expired at this point on the outside, or perhaps not (I still do not know if I am able to perish).

Use these writings to acquaint yourself with this place—I've bequeathed this to you for this express reason. You are the guardian of this place now. Protect it with your life.

We'll see the stars together.

I am going to see the world. Good Luck.

 Sincerely yours,
The Former Librarian.

And Jack!!!

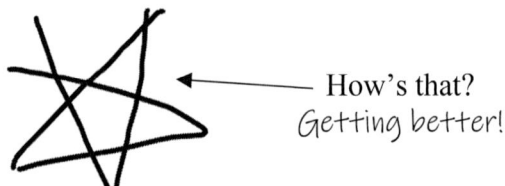

How's that? Getting better!

Eyes Are Windows

Edith took great pride in being a mother. Her son was a fine young boy, regardless of whatever rumors the people in their little town came up with. Like all other children, he was a troublemaker, but he wasn't too rude, and Edith was the type of mother to curb those sorts of manners out of him before they became a problem. Her son was curious about the world, but he would be kind. Inquisitive, but cautious. Learning, but gentle.

Her boy was the special sort, and not in the way that parents were supposed to tell their kids that they were so. Edith knew when she took him in that she needed to be prepared for anything that came with raising children. She hadn't expected magic, but then again, it wasn't like there were baby books on that sort of thing. Whatever her child's gifts were, she had promised to nurture them to the best of her ability.

It broke her heart to know that other people would never see her son the way she did.

There was crying coming from the bathroom.

Edith gently knocked on the door. "Jove? Do you want someone to talk to or do you want alone time?"

When she didn't hear an answer, she cracked the door open, taking a quick peek inside. Jove was sitting in the corner, his knees pulled up to his chest, head bent. Edith was, by now, used to the strange things that happened around her son when he got emotional. He was still a child, after all, still learning how to deal with his emotions. Add magic to that, and you were bound to get some…*interesting* side effects. There were instances of all their silverware being bent into odd shapes and objects moving about where they shouldn't, but when Jove got really upset, there were mushrooms. Edith could see them now, growing out of his exposed arms and legs, ones of different colors and of all sorts of shapes and sizes. She knew he hated them and that sprouting them would only make his mood worse, which would make them grow larger and make him sprout more, the cycle continuing over and over until he calmed down.

He didn't raise his head at the sound of her cane across the tile floor as she neared, easing herself to sit on top of the closed toilet seat.

"Jovie, what's wrong?" She placed a gentle hand on his shoulder. He tensed up.

"Mama?" Her boy sounded so small, so scared when he looked up at her. His eyes were like static, a shifting, changing haze, the marks of tears staining his cheeks. Edith didn't like seeing her son like this, knowing that his eyes only changed like that when he was confused, tired, and angry. His eyes told her so much, but she still wanted to know, wanted to hear her son talk to her about what he was feeling. She wanted him to know that it was okay and that he could speak to her about anything that had happened to him. "What am I?"

She really wished she could just say, *you're my son,* and that would soothe his worries, make his pain go away, but that was not what he meant, not what he wanted. "I don't know, sweetheart, but that doesn't matter, okay? Did someone say something to you at school?"

"They were making fun of my eyes again," he murmured, rubbing at his face. "They keep calling me a demon."

"So what if you're a demon?" It was entirely possible. He probably wasn't, but Edith wasn't going to rule out anything until she was completely sure. "I don't mind."

"You're my mother. You're not supposed to."

She sighed. "You're a good boy, sweetheart. That's all that matters, and I know it's frustrating not knowing things about yourself, but that doesn't make what other people say about you right. Your eyes are beautiful. *You're beautiful.* I'll have another talk with your teacher, see what she can do, alright? But in the meantime, I know what those other kids say about you hurts, but you shouldn't let it get to you. There are some people who are always going to be mean, no matter what. Stay with your friends; let them know there's something bothering you. They're not putting their hands on you, are they?"

"No," He muttered something under his breath.

"What was that?"

"They think…I'll curse them."

"I think I'm going to talk to the principal as well." Edith shook her head. This wasn't right. Even if her boy wasn't human, it still wasn't right. He had such a good heart, such a kind soul. Edith didn't quite care *what* he was, just as long as she could raise him right. She wished she could know more about him, about what she could do for him, but there wasn't much. Research on magic and otherworldly creatures—trustworthy sources—were few and far between, going off of what "felt right" according to her boy, and none of them could narrow down what Jove was. And while it wouldn't stop other kids from outright bullying him, it might have brought him some peace to know what he was, and where he came from. Jove loved his magic, his gifts, but on days like this one, it was often hard for him to accept it.

"Do you want to talk about it, or do you want a distraction?"

Jove took a deep breath, again wiping his eyes. "Distraction."

"Alright. A little birdie told me we have enough things to make cookies, and I could use some help."

"Chocolate chip?"

"Are there any other kind?" she joked. "We can bake, but let's get you cleaned up first, okay? Up on the counter."

Jove made a whimpering noise as he shuffled to get up, clearly still not okay.

"You're allowed to cry, honey."

"But I don't want to."

She hugged him as she stood. "I know, darling, I know."

Jove watched her, sniffling, as she rooted around the drawers for the clippers.

"They don't hurt, do they?" she asked, as she did each time they did this, just in case. Jove shook his head. "And it doesn't hurt to trim them?"

"No."

"Good." She sighed. "Good."

She began to get to work, snipping off whatever she could while trying not to cut into skin. There was a very fine line between mushroom and flesh, and while she'd gotten used to doing this, she was also able to make mistakes, so she tried her best to be careful. Unlike her paleness, her son's skin was a beautiful brown in color, with lighter patches in places. Edith remembered having a long talk with Jove before he started school, that if someone had made fun of him for the way he looked, he needed to tell her immediately, but the only thing that was said was about his eyes, about how they looked like a demon's, about how he was not normal.

If Edith could wrap her boy in a warm blanket and protect him from the world, she would, but she couldn't.

"What do you say to mushroom stew for dinner?" she asked, holding up a white mushroom that she had cut free.

Jove made a face. "Ew!"

"I'm only kidding. We'll compost them—be good for the backyard." The joke, along with the prospect of sweets, seemed to brighten his mood a little bit. She'd do more later, see if he wanted to watch a movie or something, and write a note to his teacher that he couldn't get his homework done. The static in his eyes was beginning to fade, and the natural blood-red of his irises returning. He'd been born with those eyes, and it felt strange to cover them up not only when everyone knew what color they were, but she didn't want her boy to think that he should hide himself away, cover himself up. That would solve nothing. Those kids would still make fun of him, and they wouldn't change. Her son would come home from school again, crying, because he hated himself, hated the way he looked, hated what he was, whatever that may be.

As she wiped her son's face with a warm cloth, she knew she was going to raise hell at that school. It wasn't the first time she'd gone in for chats, and she knew that children…well, they were children, so sometimes they didn't know what they were saying. It was time to stop being nice. These kids were making her boy miserable.

But now was not the time to think about that. They had cookies to bake.

"Get the mixer, dear." She paused as she opened the drawer with the measuring cups and spoons, holding up the twisted set of cutlery. "Jovie."

"Sorry, Mama." His gaze dropped to the floor, ashamed.

She patted him on the head, handing the spoons to him. "Just set them straight again."

He stared at her outstretched hand, crossing his eyes, his tongue poking out of the side of his mouth as he concentrated. The spoons began to unstick themselves, furling out like flowers in bloom.

"One day you better hope to figure out how to do that without making such a face. It'll get stuck like that."

"Nuh-uh!" he boasted.

"Yuh-huh. My daddy once pulled a face, and it got stuck like that. We had to have a closed-casket funeral because of it."

"That's a lie!" he said as he unstuck the rest of the forks and knives, his voice pitching upwards and his eyes flickering green for a moment. Edith couldn't place why metal of all things, why that seemed to be the first thing that went screwy, no pun intended, but she was just glad he didn't cause a pipe burst or anything too big for him to fix. She made a note to see if Jove would be interested in welding or things like that when he got a bit older. It might convince him that his powers weren't so bad after all if he learned how to do something with them.

It did worry her, though, having a child like Jove. She wondered if her boy would be snatched away, called to some greater purpose, like in books or movies. She feared her son would be *that special someone* and that she'd never see her child again. She fretted, wondering if each day with him would be her last. Knowing that magic was supposedly common—common but well-hidden unless one knew where to look—it calmed her to know there were other gifted people. Not similar, because Jove seemed one of a kind, but close enough. There were people out there who wouldn't blink twice at this magic nonsense. Her boy wasn't the only one, meaning he wasn't special on that account.

He was special *to her.*

Edith watched as her child, her boy, her everything, screwed up his face again and smiled as he made the mixer turn on without it being plugged in, the metal parts moving by his will.

He'd be alright. She knew that deep down. Her boy would turn out just fine, and she'd make sure of it.

She pulled him into a tight hug, kissing him on the top of his head. "I love you, baby."

"Love you, Mama," he murmured into her shoulder.

"Good. Do you wanna crack the eggs?"

"Mmhmm."

"I'll get a bowl." She didn't move for a moment, frowning at herself. "Jovie, what do we do if someone says something mean to you?"

"Ignore it and spend time with friends," he said, repeating what she had said earlier.

"And if they lay their hands on you?" Edith asked, just to make sure.

"Don't take no shit and swing back," he said without hesitation. "Fuck them up and make them regret it."

"Jovial William Croft," she scoffed, but there was no bite to it, "you have quite the mouth on you."

"I got it from my mama," he said proudly, giving her a toothy smile.

Edith laughed. "That you did."

Made of Stone

Athena was afraid of snakes. They were disgusting and slimy, and when she was younger, they did a demonstration at school where one had unhinged its jaws and swallowed a rat whole, and she had cried about it for days afterward. If she thought about it too hard, she would start crying about it again. That poor rat! It hadn't deserved to die, certainly not right in front of Athena! She shuddered thinking about it, even though it had quite literally happened years ago. It was still fresh in her mind, just as it had been when she first saw it, and she was frequently visited by nightmares where instead of a rat, she was swallowed whole by a fanged, gaping maw.

She was reminded of that instance every time she went to work, with the company's insignia emblazoned with the coiled image of a snake ready to strike. Although having seen it every day since she started working here, it still unnerved her, as if the bronze carving would suddenly spring to life and take her as its first target.

Apparently, the founder of the company loved snakes, and so it became their symbol. Athena didn't see the point in it. The people that came to them were looking for a safe place, and she wasn't exactly sure the many, *many* images of serpents ready to strike were the best idea to make them feel safe or welcomed, but no one else had complained about it as far as she knew, so it was just her.

It was...something she had needed to get used to, but it still creeped her out, feeling like the dead eyes of the animal were always staring at her. She could at least say that she could sit in her office and file paperwork with the logo gaping at her from where it was painted on the closed door and not feel complete dread.

The logo didn't matter anyway. She loved her job, and she knew it was good work. Helping people had always been something she had wanted to do ever since she was young, and with the Aegis Foundation, she could actually see the benefits of their work. She knew where every single penny went, and she knew it was all for the people that they were meant to keep safe, to help them recover from whatever life had thrown their way. Athena oversaw a lot of the process, from showing their residents to their new lodgings to dealing with the inner workings of keeping the company afloat.

Would she still work here if it dealt with dealing with *actual* snakes?

Ehhhhhhh.

The shelter house took the shape of a luxury apartment building, bought out by Medo, a young woman from old money whose family had apparently made their fortune through the fashion industry in the south of Europe. The funds for the start-up were made from that fortune; the rest of the money was produced by the fashion line and funneled into the shelter—which doubled as their agency—and paying its staff. She was reclusive, and it wasn't often that she showed herself in public, her media team dealing with the press and anything that should arise, not even bothering to show her face for her own fashion shows. Apparently, this was for the best because Medo was someone you did not want to upset. She was apparently just as cutthroat as she was kind.

Athena was newer than a lot of the other staff, but she had heard horror stories about the renovation of the building when Medo had taken over—the scandal that the construction company had cut corners when it came to the reno, causing a lot of mishaps for the people that had lived there. The company in question still claimed it was Medo's poor design that was to blame and that she herself had called for such shortcuts, despite the evidence against them and the fact that they very publicly lost the court case, with other clientele coming forward with similar instances.

There was a rumor that one of the decorative statues in the founder's office was some poor construction worker who had threatened Medo and her company and had been stuffed into a cement mixer. It was just a rumor, of course, but in the early days of the company, it was blown up enough that it led to a police investigation that had gone nowhere. The statue was 100% stone, and although someone from the company had gone missing, none of it had to do with the founder. Apparently, he'd run away with his mistress and had moved to Hawaii and was not encased in cement like everyone thought he was.

Still, that didn't stop people from believing that there was some greater conspiracy going on. Athena had, on multiple occasions, to deal with strange protestors who would stand outside their building, harassing the people that lived and worked there, yelling at them that they were 'blind to the truth' or some other nonsense. That the construction company had been right, that the missing man was up in Medo's office as proof of her cruelty, that there was something wrong with her and her organization as a whole.

Athena knew that was bullshit.

The people that came to them were scared, and vulnerable, and often needing a place to stay after suffering from abuse. Coming to a place that had accepted them and screaming in the faces of victims that *they weren't safe* and the woman that had taken them in was *out to get them* was in poor taste at best, cruel at worst. Medo wasn't the murderous tyrant everyone painted her as, mysterious as she was. If she were, she wouldn't have spent all her money on this place and poured every last dollar into making the people that graced the foundation's hallways comfortable, making them feel like they had a home.

Athena had never met her before. Apparently, she only intervened if someone came looking for one of their tenants, often looking to drag them back to their abusive home or start a fight. Athena had only seen her from a distance, watching her stand in between the attacker and victim, telling security she would handle the issue. She must have, because Athena never saw that man again.

A mother of a friend of hers had once told her, when she was young and just learning that life was complicated and that sometimes people were wicked for no reason, that people who had suffered abuse were made of stone. That they did what they needed to do in order to protect themselves, and sometimes that meant letting themselves turn to stone, letting themselves be worried about softening up just a little as they felt as if they weren't safe, that the moment they turned to flesh again something would hurt them. The woman she knew as Hera had told her that sometimes it was necessary for people to turn to stone, but it was also important to remember that it would change over time. Hera told her that she'd feel less like a chunk of stone—unmoving, heavy and burdened, stuck—and more like a person again. She just needed to give it time to rest, to heal. Athena had seen it time and time again. She'd seen people who wouldn't say a word to her, slam the door in her face, or cower from her give her a hug and thank her as they moved out of the shelter and to a more permanent place to stay, moving on with their lives. She'd seen people who would shut themselves away open up again, seeing people smile for the first time in years.

Her job was mostly behind a desk, dealing with finances and other such matters, yes, but she did enjoy work that was more direct from time to time—making beds and cleaning rooms, serving food in the cafeteria, lending an ear when residents wanted to talk but were not ready to speak to a counselor, or just wanted someone impartial. It felt nice to make someone's day better, even through the little things.

Still, she wondered about their founder, shut away in her office, only speaking to a select number of people, only coming out if necessary. She wondered about the woman who poured everything into helping others but did not bother to help herself.

Lee was buzzing around her office door when Athena stepped off the elevator. She was one of Medo's closest confidants, but unlike their boss, the woman was a chatterbox and loved to talk. She was the social aspect of

Aegis and spoke to the media most often. It wasn't rare for her to be fluttering around like a hummingbird, complimenting people and checking up on everyone to make sure the company was running smoothly, but now she looked incredibly nervous, shuffling from foot to foot, worrying her bottom lip through her teeth.

"What's up?"

"Well, you didn't hear it from me, but Sissy and Medo are coming down for an inspection."

Sissy—that's what Lee called her, but Athena wasn't sure of her real name, and she wasn't sure if anyone else knew it either—was Medo's other confidant. She handled all the legal matters and basically ran the company like a tight ship. If something was wrong, you went to her, and you prayed to whatever god that she was in a good mood. She wasn't an angry woman, but apparently, her stare could take even the most courageous down a few pegs.

"Surprise inspection," Athena repeated, chewing on the inside of her cheek. Sissy often did inspections to make sure everyone was doing what they were supposed to. To have Medo with her meant that someone had royally fucked up. And while Athena was sure that the mistake wasn't on her, there was a small seed of doubt that was beginning to settle.

"It *was* supposed to be a surprise inspection," came a voice from behind her, Sissy leveling her counterpart with a glare, making Lee back away as the rest of the floor collectively froze, all taking in the rare sight of their boss.

Athena wasn't sure if she'd seen all three women in the same place at once, but looking at them now, she wondered if the green headscarves were a choice to make them look more uniform. Medo standing before her, Athena's face reflected in her mirrored sunglasses.

She nervously swallowed, even though she knew—as far as she was aware—that she had done nothing wrong.

"You. What's your name?"

"Athena."

"Huh." Her boss cocked her head to the side, mirrored sunglasses leaving her unreadable. "I hate that name."

"Picked it myself," she mumbled, not quite sure how to respond to that. She supposed locking oneself away from most people would make them lose a few social skills.

Medo's expression did not change. "Make it mean something, then."

Athena bit her tongue. She wanted to say that her name *did* mean something to her, that she picked the name of the goddess of wisdom and battle strategy to show that she was a different person from who she had been before, that she was older, wiser, and had come out of her past battles victorious, much like the many residents they took in. But at the end of the day, this was still her superior, and she did not need to lose her wonderful job because one person didn't like her name.

"Accountant," Sissy helpfully supplied. "Not what we're here for."

Athena retreated into the safety of her office as Sissy turned her attention to Lee, beginning to chew out the poor woman for her lack of restraint. She wouldn't get into too much trouble, too integral for the company for a minor slipup like that to put her job in danger. Athena tried to get her work done while she avoided listening in on the heated argument going on just outside her office, incredibly visible through the glass walls. She watched as Sissy pushed her counterpart along, Lee shooting Athena an apologetic look before being shuttled off, and Medo following the two without any care.

There was about half an hour before Athena saw them walk by again, ducking her head to avoid eye contact with Sissy. Lee would tell her what was going on sooner or later, but she wondered what exactly was so important that the founder had to get involved, insistent on being hands-off on nearly everything.

She felt sorry for whatever poor soul was stupid enough to piss them off.

Rising from her chair to stretch, she noticed a bag by her door, recalling that Sissy had been holding it earlier. She must have set it down while she'd been talking to Lee, forgetting to take it with her.

Athena again bit her lip. On the one hand, Medo was probably pissed. On the other hand, Sissy's work stuff was in there, so it probably wouldn't be that bad if she intruded for a moment to return something.

She'd never been in Medo's office before. She didn't think anyone but Lee, Sissy, and the unfortunate souls that had crossed her had been in there.

Medo's office was quite large, a wide space that was so large that it was not immediate to the woman that Athena had let herself in, off to the side standing behind her desk. Large, white columns made the room seem even more impressive, giving it the look of an old museum. There wasn't exactly any privacy. Once you took the elevator to the top floor, you were in Medo's office. There wasn't any waiting room or anything else where Athena could make herself scarce while the three women dealt with what Athena would assume was a firing. Lee and Sissy were standing at attention a good way away, and before Medo were two people that Athena was only vaguely familiar with. Susan and Robert worked on the same floor as her, but they were with the PR department and worked with Lee most of the time. Lee had mentioned them in a few of her gossipier conversations, but Athena was so out of their social sphere that she couldn't remember anything about them or care.

"Now what do you two have to say for yourselves?" Athena could practically feel the anger radiating off of her and the poison in her tone and was suddenly glad that she wasn't immediately visible and that Medo's attention was not on her.

"I don't understand why I'm here," Susan said, awkwardly clearing her throat.

"I don't either."

Medo snapped her fingers, and Sissy pulled out a file from one of the cabinets behind the desk, handing it to her with swift precision, almost as if they'd been practicing the maneuver.

"I have no less than…oh my, twelve accounts of stolen personal items belonging to residents here. Let's see. Charlotte's watch, Phill's wedding ring, Dominique's earrings…should I go on?" The file aggressively snapped shut. "I would have liked to have dealt with this situation sooner, but you two covering for each other does make things difficult. Looking past that, I've had quite a few complaints from residents about your treatment with them. Which should we talk about first?"

"I—" Susan tried to speak up.

"And don't lie to me."

"It was Susan's idea," Robert blurted out.

"You son of a bitch!" She lunged at him, only to be held back by Lee as Robert took a few steps back to get out of range of her kicking legs and swinging arms.

Medo banged her hands on her desk, and they both went silent. "You're not children, so I expect you two to act like adults. Blaming one another? Really? You think that's a viable excuse for stealing from hurt, vulnerable people?"

"Yes," Susan admitted, hissing the answer through clenched teeth. Athena couldn't even move; sure she was watching something that was not meant for her eyes.

"Did you think that you're entitled to a higher pay, at the expense of other people's suffering?"

"I've worked for this company for over a decade," she spat, breaking free of Lee and Sissy's hold. "I've never gotten any thanks, any raise, any sort of recognition. I'm only taking what I'm owed."

"I pay you fairly," Medo said, annoyance creeping into her tone. "I pay every single worker here everything they need and then some. You have benefits, a very comfy paycheque, and perhaps if you were actually deserving of a raise, I would have granted you one. But even before you became violent, my eyes say that all you've done for these past ten years was gripe and moan about how this work, how helping people, is beneath you. You should have been fired years ago, and it is a grievous error on my part for thinking you'd grow out of that behavior after lecturing."

She turned to Robert. "And you. Do you honestly think that shifting the blame onto someone else would absolve you of all of this? That's…pathetic. Blackmailing them to keep them quiet, physically and verbally abusing them—I really wish I was able to do something about this earlier, but the two of you have made things quite hard for the people that actually want to do good at this company. The people in our care come here to be safe, and to get away from things that people like *you* do to them. The fact that it was able to go on for this long is shameful, and the two of you are disgusting. Get your things, get off my property, and prepare to hear from my lawyers."

They started toward the door.

"Actually." Whatever anger Medo was holding disappeared almost immediately, her cheery voice turning sickeningly sweet. "I have a better idea."

She walked around the desk, getting a better look at the pair.

"The two of you," Medo said, studying them intensely even behind those shades, "would make excellent models. I'll tell you what—model for me, and I won't bring this up again."

Robert cocked his head to the side. "Really?"

Athena couldn't believe it either. All those rumors about how harsh Medo was toward people who had wronged her, and these two were going to be let off the hook for all the damage they'd done?

She felt angry. That couldn't be it, right? These two had hurt people and abused their power over them when it was their job to protect them and make them feel safe, and they were going to get away with it with a mere slap on the wrist?

What the fuck?!

Before Athena could burst out of her hiding spot, scream and shout, and threaten to go to the press with this, claiming that those people at the front doors had been right all along, Medo clapped her hands together.

"Yes! You two would be lovely models! Euryale, Stheno—help position them. I know just what to do."

Athena watched Lee and Sissy, Euryale and Stheno, apparently, practically materialize at their sides, holding them in place, roughly moving them into various poses, looking to Medo for approval.

"Arms higher, Euryale. Tilt his head to the side. Yes! That's it."

They were shuffled in such a way that Athena could no longer see Medo from where she was standing, only her sunglasses in her hand by her side. Lee and Sissy turned their heads away from her.

"That's it," she said again, still in that sing-song voice. "Stay like that. Now—smile!"

Susan and Robert froze. They stopped moving, and Athena could only watch, mouth agape, as *something* raced across their skin, permanently sticking them in place as they no longer moved. Lee and Sissy stepped back, Medo placed her glasses back on, and Athena could only stare as everything in her screamed at her to run. Her co-workers weren't moving anymore; they had been encased in stone. Unmoving, unbreathing, dead. Dead in an instant. Dead before she could blink.

She dropped the bag, and all three heads turned toward her.

Athena bolted toward the elevator.

Something slammed into her before she could press the button, her fingers merely an inch away.

"Sorry!" Lee shrieked at her as they both tumbled to the floor, trying to pin Athena down as she thrashed and kicked and screamed. Athena tried to grab at her, at something, anything that would give her the upper hand. Her hand landed on the headscarf, tugging it and hopefully pulling it free so she could —she didn't know what. Blind her? Grab at her hair? All that was fueling her was panic, and she didn't have that many options.

The sound of hissing filled her ears, and Athena screamed.

The writhing mass that sat atop Lee's head hissed and lunged, biting at her as she raised her arms to protect her face.

Lee pulled away from her, reaching toward the discarded scarf, and Athena scrambled to her feet. Snakes, those were snakes. Why—how—what—

She didn't fucking care. She just needed to get out of here.

And realized she couldn't, all three women blocking the elevator, all three of them with near identical nests of vipers.

Athena fumbled through her pockets, looking for something to defend herself with, coming up empty as she realized anything she could have used to protect herself was in her purse, back downstairs in her office.

All she had was a single pen, which she brandished like a weapon with trembling hands as she cried and whimpered. This was the end.

Medo stepped toward her, plucking the pen from her hand, and Athena squeezed her eyes shut tightly. If she didn't see it, the danger was gone. If she didn't see it, the danger was gone. If she didn't see it, the danger was gone. If she didn't see it, the danger was gone. If she didn't see it, the danger was gone—

"Open your eyes." There wasn't any malice, but Athena knew this trick; she knew it was a ploy to get her to listen, and she screwed them shut tighter. "Athena, was it? You've done nothing wrong. I'm not going to hurt you. Please, open your eyes."

Athena resigned herself to her fate. Slowly opening her eyes, Medo stood in front of her, but all she saw was her own reflection in mirrored sunglasses. There was still the issue with the snakes, still moving and wriggling about, but they stayed put, less hostile than before.

Athena whimpered, flinching as Medo took her hand.

"I promise you that I will explain everything, and that you're safe, alright? You just…came in at an inopportune time. You haven't done anything wrong, okay? You're alright."

She nodded.

"Why are you crying?"

Athena could only blubber.

"What?"

"I'm—I'm scared of—of snakes."

Medo paused, looking at her from behind those glasses. Then laughed.

Calm Waters

It took five baths for 713 to become clean, and even before that, it had taken a lot of work.

The metal segments that kept his back upright, straight as a rod, preventing him from slouching, had taken several minutes of Edric trying to get the rusted bolts, the metal collar connected to them, along with the other metal partitions that lined his limbs and torso, to budge. When those parts had finally fallen to the floor, 713 was unsure if he should stop Edric—they were both going to get into trouble, but Edric was looking at him with something that 713 could only liken to the way a cat mewled when one stepped on its tail with heavy boots, and no one had ever looked at him like that before, pained like that.

The metal supports had been made to never be removed from the suits. They'd always come together. There were moments where the suit needed to be removed out of necessity, but other than that, it stayed put. If 713 was fortunate enough to perform his job well enough to be gifted a new suit, the supports would be built in, and he would have to go see a handler for the old ones to be removed and the worn materials scrapped. 713 had only been given the luxury once before, and he couldn't remember when that was, but the similarities between the experience and Edric's process ended after the man had managed to thoroughly strip him.

Edric had to cut into the waterproof canvas of his worker's suit in order to pull the fabric away from his skin. The sweat-soaked material stuck to him, digging into him as it was pulled away, leaving his skin a bit raw, and it hurt a little bit. Edric was muttering about something called a 'carpet burn'. This carpet burn wasn't so bad. Certainly, the fleas were worse with their picking and biting and scratching. Edric didn't seem to like them either, staring at him open-mouthed for a moment before his face contorted and he pressed his nose in the crook of his elbow, backing away from him.

"I—" he coughed. "I'm going to have to cut all that off."

713 cocked his head to the side in a silent question.

"Your hair. Can't you smell—never mind. It's full of mold."

Mold. Oh, that wasn't any good. Master Benton hated for there to be mold. 713 once had to clean it out of a corner of the pantry, tossing out all the food that had spoiled and prying away the infested shelves, replacing them with cleaner, healthier wooden planks that would surely hold much better than the rotten ones ever could. It had taken him a while to get rid of it all, tucked into the back of the cramped space. How in the world did it get into his hair? Was there a hole in his suit that some had gotten into, and he hadn't noticed?

"I can't clean that out," he went on. "There's too much. I'll have to cut it off."

713 didn't need to consider his options. The mold was a hazard and needed to be gone. He nodded. He wasn't sure if he'd ever had a haircut before. It didn't seem to hurt from what he'd seen. The barber shop in town seemed pleasant, always full of chatter when he happened to pass by.

"Hold on. There's something I need to go get. Can you wait here?" 713 nodded. "I'm going to lock the door so no one else will come in, okay?"

Honestly, it didn't feel like Edric had taken too long. While 713 was waiting, he passed the time by playing his favorite game, Count How Many Tiles There Are. His second favorite game was How Many Planks Of Wood Are There, followed closely at number three by How Many Numbers Can I Count To Before This Chore is Done. The games were similar, but 713 preferred to count tiles. Tiles were square, even, and more satisfying to count than wood planks, and just counting numbers wasn't as fun as counting objects.

He'd counted 498 by the time Edric had come back. Well, actually, he'd counted 498 before he decided he was bored and then caught a glimpse of himself in the mirror. The face that stared back at him was unfamiliar, but before he could study it more clearly, Edric had returned.

"Alright, buddy, I've got some things I think'll be helpful for this." He held up his bag full of spoils, 713 unable to discern what was in it, a bit too preoccupied with the thought of whether he'd ever, in all the years they'd known each other, he'd told Edric his name. Had he? When was the last time he'd spoken? Had he ever spoken? Could he speak?

No. He didn't think he could. He wasn't supposed to, anyway.

"Can I ask you something? What's the longest you've been out of your suit for?"

713 held up his hands.

"Ten?" 713 nodded. "Ten what? Days?"

713 held his thumb and pointer finger close together.

"Hours?" Edric's face paled as he pinched his fingers closer together. *"Minutes?"*

713 nodded again.

"What for?"

He pointed to his mouth, then between his legs. Five minutes to eat and five minutes to go to the bathroom, three times a day. 713 had managed to get into the habit where it only took three minutes to do each, leaving four minutes for him to try to pick at the fleas and scratch at his itchy skin, but it was hard to do so when the handler wanted him to go back to work. If he took less than ten minutes, the suit would be put back on, and he'd be sent out to work again. If he took longer, they'd take whatever food he hadn't eaten away.

"Okay." Edric took a deep breath. "Okay."

He stepped behind him, holding up the scissors, 713 watching his movements in the mirror. A hand came to rest on his shoulder, and 713 immediately jumped away from him. It hadn't hurt; it was just…surprising. It felt strange. It was different from his own hands, or the constant touch of fabric. Just being out of his suit made him feel nervous, the cool air around him brushing up against bare skin and making him shiver, but the touch was something else entirely.

"Sorry!" Edric pulled his hand away. "Sorry, I…I just—sorry!"

713 slowly relaxed his shoulders, inching back toward the other man. Edric had always been kind to him. No one else really gave the Masks like him the time of day, much less took him to get patched up when he was injured. Edric had picked him up when he'd collapsed, had roused him gently to ask if he was alright, insistent that he check him over for injuries, making sure that he was okay, and 713, who hadn't wanted to refuse Edric's kindness, had been inclined to agree, but now he was thinking of what would happen if Master Benton—Edric's father—happened upon them. This was a punishable offense, regardless of whether or not Edric had instigated this. The metal supports of his suit were broken, and his handlers would not be inclined to grant him a new one. He was going to be in *so much* trouble.

But Edric was looking at him again as if he were a wounded puppy, and 713 felt a pang of guilt in his stomach. Edric went through all this trouble to see if he was okay. He didn't want to waste all of that work, so he'd play along with this for just a little while longer, just until the mold was gone.

713 anticipated the touch this time, but he still flinched anyway. Edric seemed to realize that, keeping the scissors away from him until he'd adjusted.

"Hold still."

713 watched his hair come away in chunks, watched it in the mirror as it fell to the floor, his head feeling lighter with each *snip, snip, snip* of the scissors. When Edric was finished, 713 ran his hand through it, marveling at the prickly but not unpleasant feeling of it underneath his

fingers. He didn't feel like he was craning his neck upwards anymore either, his hair nearly all gone.

The first bath was simple. 713 knew what baths were, as he'd drawn many for Master Benton in his time working at the estate. Not in this room in particular. This was Edric's bathroom, and Edric had never asked him to draw him a bath, although it was a part of 713's job to make sure that the bathrooms were clean. It looked quite similar to Master Benton's, the white and gold prim and proper, 713 feeling a little smug at his work.

713 hadn't expected the bath to be for him and was quite surprised when Edric took him by the hand and led him into the waiting warm water. It felt nice, to be honest, yet another strange sensation. When the Masks washed themselves, they were never so exposed like this, 713 sloshing the water back and forth with his hands, playing with it, tracing his fingers along the surface.

Edric sat outside the tub next to him, watching him intently.

"Can I touch you?" Edric slowly held out his hand to him. "Would that be alright?"

Touch was still awkward, still strange, but Edric was careful, and he obviously didn't mean any harm, so he supposed that it would be alright, just for now.

Edric began to scrub the soap into his skin. 713 had used soap before. He was required to wash his hands after he used the bathroom, but that was about it. There were also the special soaps used to clean the suits, but those always smelled weird, even through his mask, too clinical, too sanitized. The soap Edric was using had a light smell that he couldn't place, but 713 liked it. He liked soap. Washing his hands intrigued him, and it had always been delightful, the same thing now with the washing of the rest of him. He still tensed at Edric's touch, but again, it wasn't bad, just foreign. Edric was actually very gentle, especially when 713 squirmed when his hands grazed a sensitive spot. Edric would pull away, as if it hurt, would avoid that spot and try again later. 713 slowly grew accustomed to this, to someone else's hands on him. The soap stung where the fleas had bitten him, but it was no worse than the flea bites themselves, so he couldn't really complain about it.

Baths were nice, he decided, as Edric softly ran more soap—shampoo, Edric had called it—through what little hair remained, nails against his scalp. Water from a pitcher was poured over his head, with Edric telling him to close his eyes, rinsing out his hair.

The second bath wasn't actually a bath at all. Edric drained the near-black water, and more pitchers were poured over him to get rid of the dirty suds that still clung to his body, 713 running his hands over his arms in bewilderment. So much dirt, and he hadn't even realized! And now it was slowly being stripped away—his skin had never looked so…so…pink? Pale? Strange, strange indeed.

"Out, please." Edric rinsed the tub out as well, 713 swatting at the fleas that still picked at his skin. The face in the mirror was still unfamiliar, but he supposed that it was his.

The third bath was similar to the first, except this time Edric took a vial of something out of his bag of things and poured it into the tub, turning the water green. It smelt like…713 could quite place the smell, but gods, it was strong. Perhaps that was the way it was, perhaps it was because he wasn't used to these sensations without his mask, without his suit. Whatever the reason, it smelled incredibly bitter. Sharp, almost medicinal. It must have been another type of soap because this one also stung as he lowered himself back into the water, air hissing past his teeth.

So many baths in one day. Huh. He didn't know why Edric was doing this. Maybe because he didn't know when he'd get to take a bath again, if at all?

713 watched as Edric took the time to clean up the bathroom. Hair and scraps of fabric went into the trash, the trash taken out—that was usually his job, but he supposed someone had to do it if 713 was in the bath. That was nice of him. He really should thank him somehow after today was done. Edric held the metal supports in his hands, turning them over and studying them before setting them aside. He wouldn't know where to send them for scrapping, 713 realized. He'd do it later, but…no, he couldn't possibly. He'd get in so much trouble, but it wasn't like the suit was usable anymore.

He kept thinking about it as he watched small, dark flecks of *something* began to crop up in the colored water. It took him a moment to realize that they were fleas, dead fleas. Oh. That would be nice, no more scratching, no more itching.

Instead of more scrubbing, Edric also stripped himself, sitting at the opposite end of the tub, taking a deep breath, and dunking his head underneath. It was ridiculously large, the tub, enough to fit even more people inside. 713 supposed it was a smart idea. If Edric got fleas from him, Master Benton would never forgive him. 713 followed suit, also dunking his head under the water, getting every bit of him wet, and being thorough even though he didn't like his head being underwater, his eyes now stinging.

The tub was drained again, and the fourth bath was more scrubbing, this time with something that smelled very pretty, much better than the green water, and much sweeter than the soap from the first bath.

Edric now had a towel wrapped around his waist, continuing his process. 713 had to think if he'd ever seen another person naked before. Handlers usually changed out their suits or gave them off-time in solitude. He didn't think he'd ever seen another Mask undressed.

713 turned around mid-scrub, a thick layer of shampoo coating his scalp.

"Something wrong?"

He tapped on the bottle Edric was holding, then tapped Edric on the nose.

"What does it smell like?"

713 nodded, smiling.

"Lavender."

Lavender? Like the flower? Flowers had smells? Oh wow. *Wow.* This was amazing! He'd have to check that out next time he was allowed in the gardens. It smelled so wonderfully.

The fifth bath also wasn't a bath, but it might as well have been with the number of salves and creams Edric was rubbing into his skin. He'd been dried off with a towel first, and it was much softer than what his suit had been made out of. 713 almost wanted to rub it against his face. He'd been so entranced by it that he'd barely noticed that Edric had gathered the other things from his bag, pouring a generous amount of ointment into his palm. The fleas had left their marks, and Edric was apparently hellbent on touching those marks, covering each and every single one of them up until half of his body was covered with bandages.

"Here." Edric had led him back into the bedroom, handing him new clothes. They were also quite soft, and 713 wasn't used to the way they loosely hung about his body. But it was soft, and it felt nice, and 713 supposed he must've done really well at his job if Edric was giving him new clothes.

New suit. New suit, but not a *suit.* He somewhat felt more exposed in the shorts and t-shirt than he had naked in the bath, he was so used to being covered up. Edric had also clipped his nails, which had been weird, picking the remaining dirt out from underneath them, but there seemed to be bits that were just stuck there. He really didn't like it when Edric tried to file them down, so much so that they had to stop trying altogether.

"Can you wait here again?" Edric asked, pointing to the bed. "I'll be right back. Promise. Just—make yourself comfortable?"

713 nodded, seating himself on the bed as his friend once again left him alone. This was all very dreamlike. He wasn't quite sure what to make of it, running his hands along his arms and legs, trying not to pick at the bandages that had been placed with care. 713 felt tired, but a different kind of tired than usual. Different from the way he'd go to sleep at the end of the day. Not exactly the same as after doing a full day of chores. More like the way his muscles would ache after lifting something heavy, when the relief of setting it down would hit. Kinda like he'd been holding his

breath in and only now stopped. He didn't know why, sinking down onto the bed. He hoped Edric wouldn't be mad at him for lying down. He'd feel so bad about it—Edric had been so nice to him, and he had to ruin it by lying down and ruining his bedding. But he was just so tired.

A quick nap wouldn't hurt. The bed was warm and so very inviting.

713 did sleep. He slept, but as he'd done so, he could feel things about his body, and it bothered him. The lightness of his head, the pain in his back, the itch of where fleas had once been, the sting of ointment. 713 had always slept on his stomach because of the supports, but without them, his back *hurt* and his body was bending in ways it hadn't before.

He woke up tired, with Edric lying next to him. His friend was sitting up, reading, but he put his book down when he noticed that 713 had awoken.

"How do you feel?"

713 stuck his tongue out, like he'd seen children do when they were being unruly, and Edric chuckled, handing him a couple of pills, which he swallowed.

"It'll help with the pain for now. You hungry?"

His stomach rumbled. He was, actually. Judging by the lack of light from the door leading to the balcony, it was well past the dinner bell. Not like he could walk into the mess like this anyways.

There was a tray on the nightstand, and 713 scrambled to sit up as Edric presented it to him, taking a bowl for himself and handing the Mask the other. Oh—soup! 713 liked soup.

He immediately spat the spoon out of his mouth. Hot! That was hot!

"Hey, careful. You alright?"

713 rubbed his tongue over the top of his mouth in an attempt to soothe it, nodding. He was starting to come to the conclusion that his employer and his friend were just strange people. Special soaps for cleaning, soft clothes, hot soup—what next?

To his dismay, it took him a while to finish eating, carefully copying Edric and blowing on each spoonful so he wouldn't hurt himself any further. It was incredibly late by the time he was finished, scrambling toward the door but was blocked by Edric, who had wrapped his arms around him and was moving him back toward the bed.

"You're staying."

What about curfew? What about his bunk? What about check-in tomorrow morning? He didn't have a suit—he'd broken his—and he hadn't even finished all the chores he'd meant to. And he'd made a scene earlier, hadn't he, fainting like that in front of all those people? What would Master Benton say? He hoped he didn't get reassigned. He hoped he didn't get terminated. If he went back now, if he went *on his knees,* then maybe they'd be lenient on him. Edric could vouch for him, right? Edric would tell them it was his idea, right? His friend would be on his side, right?

He tried to wriggle out of Edric's grasp, but to no avail. He didn't like this touch. Definitely not. He hated it, hated this. Why wouldn't Edric just let him go?

"You can't go back there," his friend insisted, looking at him pleadingly, and 713 could only imagine what the other man was seeing—a pathetic excuse of a Mask that couldn't do his job properly. He'd get in trouble regardless, but it would be better if he went back sooner rather than later.

"Look at me." 713 only stopped thrashing at the sound of his voice, the way it was shaking. "You can't go back there. You need to—you need to stay here. *Please.* People aren't supposed to have fleas, bud. People aren't supposed to have mold growing in their hair. People aren't supposed to have years and years of dirt caked on them and be stuck inside a goddamn suit for so long that they randomly pass out from their own smell. And I'm sorry—I'm so damned sorry I didn't see what was happening before. I'm sorry I didn't help you until now, and...I don't know what to do. There's so many others like you. I don't know what to do about any of them. We can't just leave them like that—"

Edric began to tremble.

713 wasn't sure what to think about all of that. The handler had seen the fleas, seen the dirt—he wasn't the only Mask that the handler saw, and there were many more handlers than just the one. Fleas were a Mask thing. Dirt was a Mask thing. They didn't have baths.

Why...why didn't they have baths? They had rinses but those were for the suits.

His suit got a bath, and he didn't. Why?

People aren't supposed to have fleas. So why did he?

713 sunk back into the bed, thinking about all the chores he'd had to do for years and years and years. His job to get rid of the mold and draw the baths and clean and clean and clean and clean—

713 looked at his arms, at the pale skin untouched by sunlight. He looked at the soft clothes that didn't scrape

against his skin each time he moved. He looked at the comfort that Edric and Master Benton had. He looked at the remains of food that had been served to him *warm,* that hadn't been taken away, despite it being well past ten minutes. This, despite his aches that Edric had promised would go away, was a good day. 713 would have considered it the best day he'd had even before Edric had told him all those things that shouldn't be. If his friend hadn't said anything, would he have known? If Edric hadn't taken him in after his fall, would he still have gone back to work, none the wiser?

That…that wasn't fair.

Edric was crying now. If 713 could speak, he would have told Edric that he was a single person. A single person who couldn't fix every little thing about the world. A single person that had taken the time to make sure that he wasn't hurt and cleaned him up when he saw that something was wrong, even if 713 hadn't known it himself. He would have told Edric that he was kind and that he couldn't fix everything, but he was still trying, and that meant the world.

But he couldn't, so he instead took Edric's hand and squeezed it, hoping it would help.

Soul

The fire didn't do much. It was still cold, still windy, and yet it was better than nothing. It was more so a comfort rather than for warmth, hollow bones unable to feel anything at all. Not hollow in the sense of how birds had hollow bones that enabled them to fly, but hollow in the sense that they did not feel like bones. Or perhaps they did. He would not know. The fire, despite its uselessness, was not meant for show. Someone would pass by eventually and sit by him. Talk. Sleep. He did not care. Someone would fill the gap whether he was there or not, but many did not stop if there was no fire burning where they could sit, could rest. He wasn't frail, despite the fact that he appeared to be, making him look non-threatening, but there was the fact that he was alive out here and the sword by his side, that said otherwise.

The Knight himself had no cares about whether others would join him or not. If they sat, they sat; if not, they went on their way. It said something about those who sat next to him, tired and weary and needing to stop, if just for the moment. It also said something about those who continued walking, untrusting. He did not blame them because they were right to be untrusting. There was not much around here that was kind, so it was possible for the promise of a warm fire to be a trap out in the open. The one sitting next to him was quiet, like him, going through his things without acknowledging his host with anything more than a simple nod of thanks.

The Knight sat.

Kindness was a luxury not many indulged in.

"Are you human?" The other asked in a voice neither harsh nor soft. Inquisitive, but not invasive.

"No."

The other did not ask what he was, for that would be rude, especially since he was offering them a place to sit. They were all travelers, all the same, despite the danger, despite all the death and misery.

Travelers were as common in these lands as water was in others. If you were fortunate enough to find a permanent place to stay, it meant that you were too much of a hassle to remove from wherever your residence was, meaning one would surely die trying to fight you.

"You look like one."

"Lots of things look like humans," The Knight replied, throat dry from the cold. In truth, he did not know what he was, but he was sure he was not a human.

"That's true." His temporary guest was grotesque in nature, yawning, but not the worst The Knight had seen, too many eyes for his liking. Not human as well, and not passible either.

White sands kicked up around them as the winds picked up, the fire flickering for a moment or so.

"You heading anywhere in particular?" his guest asked again. "Any direction, I mean? I heard there's trouble toward the west. Not worth it if you don't have protection."

The other gestured to The Knight's sword. "Not like you seem like the type to need any."

"Mm." The sword was old, and he could not recall where he had gotten it from, only that it had been full of chips and dents when he had found it and that it had been covered in blood. Other than its disrepair, it was a reliable weapon, one that did its job of protecting its owner. It had probably passed through many hands before falling into his.

"I have to ask," his guest said as they began to pull provisions out of their bag. What it was exactly, The Knight could not tell, only that it was some sort of meat. "You seem like the type that's been traveling a while—have any tips to stay alive?"

The Knight scoffed but opened his mouth to answer regardless. "It's simple, I find."

"Out here in chaos and misery?"

"Of course." He nodded. "Keep your head down; that's the first rule."

No one bothers you if you do not seem like you are worth the trouble. If you look scared, you draw attention, but if you're confident, that's a way to end up with a target on your back. You kept quiet unless addressed, and if you had to fight, you never revealed all your tricks unless you were really desperate.

If he were an honest thing, he would have said that telling his guest all of this was a waste of time. He could tell this creature was a spoiled one, one that traveled not out of necessity like the rest of them but because they thought it was fun. Things like that didn't last too long out here.

"Keep enough food on you that you can make it to somewhere safe and stock up," he went on. "Take too little, and you'll starve. Take too much, and that's how you end up with a knife in your back. Same with water. Stay away from the west, like you said, if it's getting rough, but remember that it's still unsafe elsewhere. Just because it isn't bad doesn't mean you're safe. Be on your guard. Trust no one."

Creatures like this one, wide-eyed and hopeful… The Knight wondered how long they would stay that way, hanging onto his every word as if it were gospel.

"Never travel with anyone." The Knight pointed out into the darkness, into the sand-covered paths that were never warm no matter how much the sun shone, always cold, always making his hollow bones ache. Too dark, too cold, not enough for him to stray too far. "Other people just make for conflict over food and spoils. Do not offer to travel with anyone, no matter how nice they appear to be."

Niceness was a luxury. Kindness was a luxury few could afford, and something no one wanted to spend. There was an understanding of those during rest, but no guarantee of safety. It was best to sleep with one eye open and one hand around a weapon, just in case.

His guest nodded along with his words, but their face looked vacant as if they had stopped paying attention to him. When they had lost interest, he did not know. He himself was hungry, so he did not blame the guests for their sluggishness.

"You must be trusting," The Knight said, "for you to feel safe enough to fall asleep around me."

The creature yawned again, its maw snapping. "You've shown no intent to harm me. I don't care if you're here when I wake or not."

"But I could kill you," The Knight argued. "I could steal your things while sleeping."

"Only a fool would tell me that. I am now aware of ill intentions. I don't think you ever planned on killing me, which is why you tell me so."

The Knight shook his head. "You are sheltered; am I correct?"

"Lived in The Stacks, yes."

"So why are you out here?"

"I was bored, so I thought I'd go traveling."

"I've seen your kind. The ones that travel for no reason." The Knight shifted so that he was sitting up straighter, no longer slouching, his hollow bones cracking with the effort. "I'm fond of them, so I will tell you the three most important rules to staying alive out here."

That seemed to garner the full attention of his guest, who snapped wide awake.

"If you want to stay alive out here, you must do exactly as I say." The Knight padded the hilt of his sword. "Firstly, you must have a reliable weapon. Do you have one?"

The creature nodded, fumbling through its supplies before producing a dagger.

"Good, good. That'll do. Second, you need to learn how to lie as well as learn how to spot a lie. You fancy you're good at that?"

The creature thought about it for a moment, then nodded again.

"Excellent!" The Knight laughed, the sound as hollow as his bones, and quickly lost on the howling wind.

"Now, this is the final rule, and I daresay that this might be the most important out of all of them, you hear me, yes?"

The creature was nodding enthusiastically now, and if it bobbed its head any harder, it might come clean off.

"The most important thing you need to know is that you should never accept kindness. Out here it means nothing to nobody. It's less than worthless. Never take food unless sold to you or you find it on your own; never accept help even if you really need it; and never, ever, sit by another's fire."

The creature slowly cocked its head to the side, brow furrowing in confusion. "If you don't mind me asking—"

"I do."

"—but why did you offer me a place to rest if it goes against your rule?"

The Knight sighed, then stood, bones cracking once more as he smiled broadly at his guest, mouth splitting open far wider than it should have, revealing rows upon rows of jagged teeth, black drool spilling from his lips.

"That is because," he said, careful of his words as a tangle of shadow-like limbs burst out from under his cloak, grabbing the creature, tearing into it with no hesitation whatsoever. "I was hungry."

The thing squirmed as it was torn apart, screaming as loud as they could with their flesh being ripped off of their bones. Soon enough, the noises stopped, and The Knight surveyed over its spoils, a ball of familiar light floating up from where the corpse lay.

The Squire, from where she was hidden in the shadows a good way off, slunk up beside him. "Anything good?"

The Knight relaxed his face, looking more human now as his appendages retreated back inside his cloak, nose scrunching up in disgust. "You meat-eaters are rancid."

The Squire hopped over to where the pieces of the body lay, clicking her forked tongue. "Like eating the soul is any better. Sins taste vile."

One more limb lashed out at the light, pulling it back toward him, and he swallowed it in one gulp. "Says the thing that feasts upon things full of fluids and chunks."

The Squire only clicked her tongue again. "I do not wish to have this argument again."

"Then eat quickly before we attract any attention. We must keep moving."

The Squire rolled her eyes. The Knight kept watch for any dangers, not too keen on watching his companion eat. If it were not for the fact that she could not hunt herself, he would not partake in such a grotesque mauling. Nothing would remain when she was done.

"Are you done?" he asked, annoyed and horrified at the sounds of meat squelching and bones crunching despite the acts he had committed mere minutes ago, familiar with her eating habits.

"Yes," she answered with the same amount of venom.

"Then we should go."

The Squire disappeared back into the shadows, The Knight following close behind.

As they stepped away from the fire's light, it extinguished.

Death and Taxes

If there was something that Sasha realized early on in his life, it was that nothing was constant. Yes, there were things that arguably remained similar, but Sasha understood that there was human error. You can't make the same cup of tea twice. You might be able to recreate something like it using the same number of teaspoons of sugar that you did the day before, but there was no guarantee that those teaspoons were exactly the same. You might have filled them a little more or a little less when scooping out the sugar. That wasn't to say that Sasha didn't enjoy his tea or coffee made in a specific way and had recipes for his favorite foods that he dared not tamper with. You could still have something similar and enjoy it. When dealing with constants, the biggest offender was people themselves. Always changing, ever-shifting. Never quite the person that you once knew and willing to kill you the second it benefited them.

Sasha wasn't usually so pessimistic. *Cautious* was a more operative word because he spoke from experience. People weren't so reliable, especially if they could be persuaded with money. It was why he paid the people that worked for him well, other than the fact that it was just common decency.

His philosophy only seemed to be proven right when Tempest went missing.

He didn't care for Tempest, but most people did concern themselves with the world's top superhero. They were sentimental like that. Sasha remembered when the news broke when the media was up in arms about not being able to reach their favorite darling during that earthquake on the western coast. They'd been so angry, like squabbling children, cursing his name until they realized that he wasn't simply avoiding them and that their beloved hero was gone. It was only then that they started to get scared. It was a hot topic for a while: what would the world do without their protector? He'd watched the interviews pour in—from other heroes that knew him, from people he'd saved, from celebrities that had briefly interacted with him. All had kind words to say. All had pleas for Tempest to come back, that the world needed him.

It took Sasha three days to realize that no one was actually looking for Tempest. All those heroes worth their salt, and no one was bothering to look despite all their proclamations that he was needed, that they loved him. Arguably, three days was too long for him to have realized the obvious, but they weren't acting like he was dead yet. They just weren't looking for him, essentially labeling him as a lost cause. No one bothered to say their real thoughts out loud. They just pretended he would come back if they asked hard enough.

And Sasha had to admit that it was sad. The most beloved person in the entire world, and no one gave two shits about him when it came down to the nitty gritty. Sasha kinda hated that he was right in this situation, that people couldn't be counted on for anything.

Despite his declaration that heroes weren't as grand as they appeared to be, Sasha was curious as to where the man had gone off to, if he had vanished of his own accord, or if—huh, he never actually thought about the possibility before—the man had managed to get himself kidnapped. When it came to Tempest, not many questioned his power. He was likened to a god among men, nearly invincible, and his weaknesses unknown. Any trap he found himself in should have been easily escapable. There were supervillains who challenged him, who fought with a similar power, always defeated, but it was strange. Anyone with the balls to kidnap, or possibly kill, the most important man in the world wouldn't stay silent about it. But Tempest was kind, too kind to just disappear without saying why. He would have felt like he owed the public an explanation, even if it were for something personal like retiring.

It stank of something rotten, and it made Sasha antsy. Something wasn't right, and it made him *concerned* of all things. He was a smart man, and so was Tempest. And Sasha knew that the hero could easily handle himself, but this wasn't something he could leave alone.

Not many people thought much of Sasha. The people that worked for him liked him well enough to count on him for their paycheque, but in the friends department, Sasha would say he was lacking and that he liked it that way. You'd be aware of them and be able to monitor them, but no sentiments to get in the way of business. Nothing to cloud the mind. No connections meant no one could stab you in the back. They'd at least stab you in the front, and then you could see them coming. An unassuming appearance meant that you looked harmless enough, and he presumed that looking for someone as imposing as Tempest would trip a few alarms. Better to approach from a safer angle. Like, civilian identity angle. Not many people could say they knew a hero's secret identity, and if they could, why would they? But Sasha happened to know this one, and he was still sort of laughing to himself as he considered it. He never thought knowing Tempest's real name would ever come in handy, something he'd obviously been sworn secret too. Not that he'd ever use it for any other reason. Not like he could start kidnapping family members and the like. It was stupid anyway—why not just deal with a hero directly if you had the option to? Much scarier for a hero to come home and find a villain calmly waiting for them, perhaps making themselves a nice cup of tea. It would rattle the most seasoned heroes. Kidnapping loved ones was just so…blasé.

The apartment in which Tempest supposedly lived in, according to information gained by calling in several favors, offering several bribes, and promising several extra holiday bonuses to Neal from IT, was plain. It was in the newer, flashier part of the city, the part they put on all the brochures to ask you to come and live there while conveniently avoiding the rampant poverty a few streets away. Sasha didn't know what he was expecting, tugging on his leather gloves, and making sure his suit looked good enough. The best way to blend in was to not stand out, after all, but Tempest was a loud man, both in manner and in presence. He wouldn't have been surprised if the place had a large, neon arrow pointing to it that said "SECRET LAIR!!! TEMPEST LIVES HERE!!!!"

A man who was not Tempest opened the door. From his gathered intel, this must have been the hero's brother, who looked decidedly unperturbed at the hero's disappearance. Sasha knew grief affected people differently. It was entirely possible that this man was entirely numb on the inside, suffering even though he didn't look like it, basically scowling at him. Probably angry to be interrupted in his bereavement.

"Hi," Sasha said, straightening himself and tugging at his leather gloves. "Do I have the right apartment? I'm looking for Morgan. I'm an old friend from high school. We had plans to meet—"

"He's not here."

Sasha frowned, pretending to be confused. His eyes flicked past the man, just a little way inside the apartment. There was a carpet on the floor, a red stain sloppily covered by the edge of it, tools and cleaners spread about. Someone else might have assumed it was wine, especially knowing that this man's brother was missing, but Sasha was not someone else.

"Are you sure? I was supposed to pick him up—"

"No. Go away."

Sasha sighed, leaning in close. Best case scenario, this man was most likely trying to hold it together and not cry in front of a stranger at the apparent kidnapping of his brother, and he was just paranoid. Worst-case scenario, Tempest was in a lot more danger than Sasha had first realized. But Sasha was usually never wrong. It was why a lot of people told him he was insufferable.

"Listen, I just want to know if those idiots got the job done properly," he whispered, not once faltering, watching the expression on the man's face. "They said something about forgetting to wipe down the scene, and…god, I just need to know these bastards didn't fuck it up any more than they admitted to, got it?"

The man's face—Sasha didn't feel too bad about forgetting the man's name anymore—relaxed and seemed less annoyed.

"Yeah, it's done."

"Okay," Sasha nodded. He took a deep breath and took a quick glance down the hallway to make sure there was no one there. Grabbing Tempest's brother by the throat, it was clear that the charming asshole he'd seen on TV was the luckier of the two. Smarter, too. Who the fuck admits to a person they've never met that they're an accomplice to murder?

"Now, you're going to tell me every single tiny detail about where they took him. If I don't like what you say, I'm going to be a bit creative, and you feel quite fragile."

He definitely had no powers, this one. Easy to intimidate. Powers made people stupid. They thought they had a fighting chance because they were special, no matter what their power was. People who didn't have the same advantages knew just how breakable they were. They could never do the same feats their hero counterparts could. Maybe that's why this man sold out his brother, jealousy. Maybe he just did it for the money. Sasha didn't care why, hearing the man squeal with the barest of effort on his part.

Typical. Can't even rely on your own family.

When he was done rambling and begging to be left alone, Sasha left him cowering on the floor, right by the bloodstain. He watched this man sob and whine. He watched him cry and blubber. None of it was with remorse. All of it was fumbled pleas of *don't hurt me* and *I'll tell you everything.* Sasha hadn't even used his powers all that much, only as a display of brute force and a warning.

"People like you are the worst," he said. "You sell out the only person in your life, and then you sell out the people you paid to do it. What a pathetic thing you are. Can't even stick to the plan. I barely laid my hands on you—you're not even bruised."

"W-who the fuck are you?"

Sasha sneered down at the miserable waste, at the man who had the nerve to put out a hit on the most powerful hero the world had ever seen, who had the stupidity to trust anyone who wore a nice enough smile. How much was he used to his brother's protection that he was this cocky, this arrogant, under the belief that no one would come for him? And as much as he hated the louse, he couldn't bring himself to extinguish the useless, squandered life in front of him. He wouldn't do so.

His life wasn't worth it, for one thing. Morgan would hate him, for another.

But his eyes fell once more on that bloodstain, and the rage he felt was insurance that he would not leave him feeling safe. The box of tools proved useful, with a crowbar nearly hidden among the rest of the cleaning things. Put back in the wrong place, and Sasha couldn't help but think, as he hefted it into his grip, that it was a stroke of luck, both good and bad. Sasha stuffed a rag into the mouth of the sobbing man, snot and tears still dribbling down his face. Without any remorse—the same amount that this man had offered Tempest—he brought the tool down in a brutal strike on the man's knee.

Sasha left the crowbar next to the man as he cried out in pain, muffled wailing escaping him as his question was finally answered.

"I'm an accountant."

Following the man's instructions led Sasha to a house outside the city. None of the people there looked to be any more than common thugs. No big names, no one Sasha could recognize as someone who would benefit from offing Tempest. Most likely, they were just idiots in over their heads. Dumbasses that didn't have much of a plan besides the actual kidnapping, that thought they could just take a swing at Tempest without much planning of what they would do once they had their fun. And that was exactly what they were doing—having fun. The blood, the bruises, the broken bones, and the ripped skin were a testament to that. If it was anyone else, this would have been a dead man; no chances were taken that their target would break free. They wanted to toy with the hero, but they'd gotten overconfident. They waited too long to tell the public where he was, and now they thought they were untouchable because the heroes hadn't come for him.

But Sasha had, and there weren't any heroes around to save them.

What a shame.

When there were no other obstacles left, Sasha wiped the blood from his face. It would be a pain to get all of that out of his clothes, but it was a small price to pay. That wasn't the big issue at the moment. Tempest was still tied up, and while Sasha was tempted to test the (what appeared to be) metal restraints to know just what exactly they were made of, he backed down. Now was not the time. The chains snapped without much effort, and Tempest—unconscious and worse for the wear but still alive—very nearly collapsed to the floor, with Sasha catching him before he could do so.

Helping him to a nearby couch, Sasha couldn't help but wonder who lived here. The place wasn't exactly lavish. Less *cottage in the woods* and more *escape bunker.* Secluded either way, a place to disappear. Generic enough for anyone to come by without suspicion if they had the money. He'd have to find out later, after finding some sparse medical supplies. It wasn't much, but it would have to do. Sasha was decent enough at first aid to get Tempest patched up, but it probably wouldn't have been able to hold if the hero didn't have accelerated healing. It was pathetic considering the severity of the injuries, but it was an attempt at least. It was more of a hassle to maneuver the hero back to the car regardless, with Sasha having enough strength to lift him but Tempest was a lot larger than he was, so it was more awkward to find a way to carry him all while not jostling his slowly closing injuries.

Once Sasha made it home and had laid his new ward down in the guest room bed, stripping him of what was left of his tattered and bloodied clothes, and covering him with blankets, he couldn't help but notice how small the man looked and how vulnerable he was. He stood there, watching for what felt like just a moment, wondering how he'd ended up in this situation.

Tempest tossed and turned in his sleep but did not wake. Sasha left him, going to get himself cleaned up and trying not to take too long. He didn't want Tempest to be confused upon waking.

No, he thought to himself as he straightened his tie, affixing the metal mask upon his face. *More confusion would only agitate him further. He needs to rest.*

The hero blinked as he awoke, still somewhat disoriented as he raised his head.

"Sentinel."

"Tempest."

"I should've known you were the one behind this." Perhaps it would've been a more impactful speech if his eyes didn't look so vacant and his face still didn't look so puffy, slowly but surely healing.

"You might find this hard to believe, but I didn't kidnap you."

Tempest, Morgan, laughed. "Oh, so you *rescued me,* then? What? Feel guilty about everything you've done? Did your heart grow in size? Or did you just want to mock me?"

"You know me better than that." Sasha sighed, sitting down on the edge of the bed. He took his mask off. Morgan hadn't seen his face before, but Sasha supposed it would be better to comfort someone if they could see you, the hero watching him intently. "Are you okay?"

Morgan was silent for a while. He sat up, eyes flicking over Sasha's appearance. "Why?"

"No one else was looking for you," he shrugged. "Someone had to."

And I'm glad I did.

"You were nearly dead when I found you."

Sasha expected some sort of joke. Deflection about how he was obsessed with Tempest enough to go looking and that he'd missed him. Some witty, sarcastic remark that belonged to Saturday morning cartoons and not out of the mouth of a legitimate hero. None of that came.

"Are you okay, Morgan?" he asked again, hoping for an answer. There was only so long he could sit here in awkward silence, hoping he'd done the right thing.

"No one came," he mumbled, and Sasha had never felt sorrier. "They had the news on when—I saw. I saw all of it. All of them asking for me to come back. I kept thinking it was to stall and that someone would break down the wall at any moment and come to my rescue. All those heroes that I—that I called friends. None of them came for me. None of them *looked.*"

But you did, went unsaid.

If Sasha were a different man, he would have lied, giving him solace. But he was not a different man, so he sat there in silence, wishing he knew how to be reassuring.

"I'm sorry."

"Is…" He swallowed nervously, "is Dylan okay? *Is my brother okay?*"

"I broke his leg. He is otherwise unharmed, although you should reconsider your living arrangements."

Worry seeped out of his face, his expression returning to that blank one from before. He must have understood. Sasha wondered if he had expected it, even. The man didn't seem too surprised at the revelation. Had his relationship with his brother been that bad? Had he known, or at least expected, that something like this was coming? Had he let it happen anyway? Or was it denial?

"You may stay here if you'd like."

"Sasha," Morgan asked again. "Why did you save me?"

They weren't friends. They'd *never* been friends. They'd been two strangers with conflicting interests. A villain and a hero, their lives entwined as they made it so they'd clash whenever they could. Sasha couldn't remember when he'd learned Morgan's name or when Morgan had learned his. It just was. They weren't close, far from it. They just knew each other in a specific context, and that context involved knowing a person laid bare.

Because how else were you supposed to ruin someone without knowing them intimately? How else were you supposed to know where to drive the knife if you didn't know all the small cracks and tiny faults unseen by everyone else? This game was…well, it was a game of sorts, wasn't it? A game in which neither of them won, not truly. A game that would go on until one of them stopped. And Sasha supposed this was a good place to stop.

"I don't know," he admitted. He didn't know for sure. Was it just curiosity about who would have taken Tempest? Did he actually care about the man's well-being? If he did, would he admit to it? He truly didn't know the answer to that question, but even though Tempest's absence—*Morgan's* absence—would've made his work easier, he could not think about that possibility. He hated to admit it, but Tempest was a constant. Unreliable, ever-changing, but a constant nonetheless. Always here, even if they were on opposite sides of the board. He would be in Sasha's life as much as he was in Morgan's.

Dammit. Perhaps he did care.

They never were typical rivals, always engaged in conversation, but they weren't friendly, certainly. But they could say that they were surprisingly amicable with each other—if they weren't, Sasha would have been in prison by now, or Tempest would truly be dead. If pressed, Sasha could say they were kind, at least more than other heroes and villains. It was a sort of limbo. Not supposed to get along with each other, and yet...

Morgan was a hero. Sasha was his villain. This wasn't how it was supposed to go, but Sasha didn't want to see him like this. How pathetic of him. The greatest hero in the world here, like this, so vulnerable. Any other villain would have taken their shot.

Sasha never would. Not with him.

"Are you okay, Morgan?" He asked again, slowly taking the other's hand.

"No." It was quiet, barely a whisper as he choked back a sob. "No, I...I..."

Sasha held him as he cried, as tears dripped onto his shirt. Not that he had wanted to—Morgan had grabbed him and hadn't let go. He was being erratic and irrational, but Sasha would not say that not after he'd been through what he had. He was not as heartless as many thought him to be. Before him was a man whose world had collapsed around him, and he was the only thing left standing among the rubble. The last thing Sasha was going to do was bury him underneath that weight, not when he had been in a similar position before. He knew how helpless one could feel, even if you were the strongest person in the world, even if you were nigh invulnerable. Even rock and steel eventually eroded away when water wore them down.

Nothing was perfect. Nothing was infallible. Nothing would last forever.

Nothing was *constant.*

So Sasha held the man who had once sworn he would destroy everything he'd ever built brick by brick as he broke down, because Sasha was not as cruel as to leave him like this, so hopeless.

"You'll be okay," he whispered. "You'll be okay. I've got you, Morgan."

The kiss was desperate. Sasha didn't know what to do; his mind struggling to catch up. It was soft but sad. He could tell Morgan was barely holding it together, holding him closer, holding on to the one thing he could count on in that moment.

It didn't mean anything.

"I—I'm sorry. I don't…" He cut himself off.

"It's alright."

Morgan was panicking right now. He wasn't aware of himself, and he needed something to ground him. Sasha supposed he was that something, the only person right now who bothered to care. It wasn't exactly the most natural reaction, but he supposed that Morgan wasn't in his right mind. Erratic. Irrational. Holding on to the one thing he had left. But it was still a mistake, and Sasha would not condemn him for it, nor would he indulge. He would not be someone's constant—he couldn't be. He was not reliable; he was not constant. He could not be someone else's stability, especially for someone who was meant to shatter him.

They would ignore this and discuss what would happen when Morgan wasn't so out of it, after he had slept longer and had eaten. There was no need to bring it up. It was just a mistake, a fleeting moment of a lapse in judgment. It would not, could not, become a constant. That was not the way things were.

"Just rest for now," Sasha told him, breaking away from him as he stood again. "You might be bulletproof, but you still need to sleep. Do you want something to eat? Drink? You must be starving."

Morgan nodded, a blank look on his face, his expression unreadable.

Sasha kept his expression neutral. Years of wearing a mask, and he would not make the mistake of thinking that someone wasn't able to gauge what he was thinking. He did not want to give Morgan the impression that he was okay with the kiss, but he didn't want to shame the man either.

Still, he prodded at his lips when Morgan couldn't see him as he tried to push it out of his mind. There was a time and place for things, and it just so happened that this had neither the time nor the place. *Ever.* People were not constant. Even if Morgan believed to feel the same when he was more present, he'd get bored of him, tired. Change his mind. That was *if* this was even a possibility in the first place, *which it wasn't.*

They weren't compatible. Hero and villain. Opposites. They did not care for each other, *couldn't* do so. That was the truth in it. Even if everything and everyone fluctuated, their choices ever-changing, they were only minute changes. This situation was an outlier, an exception. They would eventually go back to what they were. Things changed, yes, but with heroes and villains, it was never anything like what you saw in movies. It wasn't the change of heart, the redemption, or the plunge into darkness. It wasn't grand epiphanies and promises to do better or oaths of revenge.

It was a couple of extra grains of sugar in the teaspoon.

This truce would last as long as it needed to, a day or so before Tempest felt better (physically, at least), a bit of time for him to find a safe place to stay away from his brother. They'd go back to doing what they did. Morgan wasn't the type to abandon people, even if their love was conditional. He'd go back to playing hero, only he'd know that he was being used, but it wouldn't stop him because that was who he was.

"Can I ask you a weird question?" Morgan asked the moment he was in view again, trayful of food being set in his lap.

"Depends on the question," he answered hesitantly.

"Do you think you made the right choice?" Tempest cocked his head to the side—no, *Morgan* cocked his head to the side the way he did when he was confused. "Saving me?"

Sasha shrugged. "I'm obviously not a hero."

"Still," Morgan argued, "you went out of your way to save me. But you don't look happy."

"I still don't know why I bothered, but I am…not opposed."

"Ah, so your face is just naturally that grumpy!"

"Be aware that you are in *my* house, and I *can* and *will* kick you out."

"Oh really?"

"Flat on your ass," Sasha deadpanned, scowling. "Still naked."

Morgan only scoffed at him, digging into his oatmeal.

"I would," Sasha found himself saying. "Save you again, I mean. I'm not an asshole."

"I'd beg to differ."

Sasha, without thinking, smacked him—a little forcefully—on the back of the head. He stared in abject horror as he realized what he'd just done.

Morgan stared back, then laughed, breaking into a wide grin. "There we go! That's the Sash I know! I was beginning to think you'd gone completely soft!"

"Idiot," Sasha murmured under his breath as he watched the hero laugh himself silly. This was familiar, he realized, as he couldn't help but smile back.

So perhaps he'd been wrong. There *were* constants.

There was Tempest and there was Sentinel.

There was Morgan and there was Sasha.